HEAD OVER HEELS

Nick prowled toward her and she took a step backward, suddenly nervous at his intent expression. When he had her backed up against the wall, she laughed nervously. "What're you doing?" He ignored her question and lowered his head to her neck. She felt his warm lips slide against her sensitive skin and she gave an involuntary shudder. "Nick—"

His tongue thrusting into her mouth silenced the feeble protest she attempted to make. With a groan, she surrendered to him. They both knew she was powerless to resist how he made her feel. At that moment, she would have followed him off a cliff, so she issued no denial when he backed her toward the bedroom, never once breaking contact with her mouth.

Also in the Danvers Series

FALL
FOR ME

A DANVERS NOVEL

SYDNEY LANDON

A SIGNET BOOK

SIGNET
Published by New American Library, a division of
Penguin Group (USA) Inc., 375 Hudson Street,
New York, New York 10014, USA
Penguin Group (Canada), 90 Eglinton Avenue East, Suite 700, Toronto,
Ontario M4P 2Y3, Canada (a division of Pearson Penguin Canada Inc.)
Penguin Books Ltd., 80 Strand, London WC2R 0RL, England
Penguin Ireland, 25 St. Stephen's Green, Dublin 2,
Ireland (a division of Penguin Books Ltd.)
Penguin Group (Australia), 707 Collins Street, Melbourne, Victoria 3008,
Australia (a division of Pearson Australia Group Pty. Ltd.)
Penguin Books India Pvt. Ltd., 11 Community Centre, Panchsheel Park,
New Delhi–110 017, India
Penguin Group (NZ), 67 Apollo Drive, Rosedale, Auckland 0632,
New Zealand (a division of Pearson New Zealand Ltd.)
Penguin Books, Rosebank Office Park, 181 Jan Smuts Avenue,
Parktown North 2193, South Africa
Penguin China, B7 Jaiming Center, 27 East Third Ring Road North,
Chaoyang District, Beijing 100020, China

Penguin Books Ltd., Registered Offices:
80 Strand, London WC2R 0RL, England

First published by Signet, an imprint of New American Library,
a division of Penguin Group (USA) Inc.

First Printing, March 2013
10 9 8 7 6 5 4 3 2 1

This book is dedicated to my wonderful husband who is my prince charming every day. I knew he was "the one" when he said, "I get you."

To my wonderful aunt Ida. Thank God for those Jackson genes!

Also, to my friends at Blue Ridge. We shared a little of everything together in the twenty-five years I was there and I will always consider you my family.

Chapter One

"You're what?"

Beth cringed as her sister's voice rang out loudly in the bar. So much for thinking she wouldn't make a scene if she told her somewhere public.

"Will you please keep it down, sis; I don't want everyone in here knowing my business."

Suzy flicked her hand as if she didn't care, but thankfully lowered her voice as she asked, "How can you be pregnant? You actually have to have sex to get pregnant, and you aren't seeing anyone. Oh, God, you didn't get frozen sperm, did you?"

If she wasn't so mortified by this conversation, Beth would have laughed at the question. "No, I wasn't artificially inseminated so I obviously had sex. I know this is somewhat of a shock to you, but I had sex!"

Now it was Suzy looking around as Beth belatedly realized her last sentence seemed to echo off the walls of the restaurant. "Okay, let's talk about this rationally. Who is the bastard and where can I find him? He took advantage of you, and now he'll suffer the consequences. Has he even offered to step up and take responsibility?"

Beth rolled her eyes and wondered if her sister was going to challenge the father of her baby to a duel next. For such a modern woman, her sister was freaking out more than she'd have thought. Clearing her throat, Beth admitted, "He doesn't know yet. I . . . haven't told him."

"Well, when are you planning on telling the man, when the kid is in college?" Suzy sat before Beth with fire flashing in her eyes. Her red hair was pulled back in a French knot and, as usual, she was on the cutting-edge style-wise. Beth always felt frumpy around her. As a former fatty, she never felt comfortable in her new, smaller clothes. She'd lost over a hundred pounds several years ago, and even though the mirror showed her one thing, she always saw her old self staring back at her. Suzy had gotten her red hair from their mother, and Beth was stuck with their father's unremarkable brown hair. Suzy was on the tall side and Beth was on the petite side. She'd always thought she'd missed out on the best family genes for sure. Realizing that her sister was staring her down, she took a breath and dove back into the fray.

"I just found out, sis, so I haven't had time to make a lot of plans. I'm trying to come to grips with it myself. I took a home pregnancy test last week and then had a blood test with my doctor. I got those results this morning. I'm pregnant. I have my first appointment in two weeks.

"Geez, you would think I'd told you I only had a month to live or something. Freak out much?"

"Don't mess with me, girl. I have the parents on speed dial. I can only imagine the horror of having this talk with them."

"You wouldn't dare," Beth whispered.

Suzy pretended to study her fingernails. "Ordinarily I wouldn't, but I'm gonna need something to work with here. So, you either start talking, or I'm going to pull our brilliant parents from whatever laboratory they're in and tell them all about their wayward child. 'Oh God, the shame, the disappointment, the heartache,'" Suzy finished dramatically.

"You suck," Beth grumbled. "All right, I'll tell you, but you have to promise me you won't overreact. I mean it, Suzy."

"Who me? I never overreact."

With a snort, Beth took a deep breath and prepared herself. She knew from experience that her sister would release hell on her when she learned what had been happening behind her back. Maybe her friend Ella was right, this might have been a very, very bad idea, but there was no turning back now.

"I met someone about six months ago. Before you ask—no, we haven't been dating this whole time. I kind of despised him at first, but God, sis, I wanted him. He makes me feel unbelievable things. He is the first man that sends me up in flames every time I see him. Just one look from him and I'm ready to rip all my clothes off and let him do whatever he wants to with me."

Suzy was staring at her in shock.

Beth left her in silence for a minute and then prodded her with her hand.

"All right, I get the whole urge-to-bang thing, but let's speed forward to the baby daddy's name. Crap, six months? Is it someone at Danvers?"

Suzy felt like she'd landed in the twilight zone. How could she not know her sister was seeing someone? Hell, not just seeing him, sleeping with him. Maybe she'd been so wrapped up in Gray that she hadn't noticed things that she normally would.

Shit! Suzy could tell by the guilty expression on Beth's face that it was indeed someone that they worked with. Damn! She'd thought the pregnancy thing was the biggest shock she was going to get, but the dreamy look that came over Beth's face as she talked about the guy was pretty close. She'd never seen her like this. Beth had never been one to date very much and she certainly had never been so completely crazy over a man before. This guy better be on the up-and-up or his days were going to be numbered.

Suzy took a deep, calming breath and studied her sister. She didn't look freaked out; she actually kind of had a glow about her. "I never see you with anyone but

Ella or Nick. Crap, they probably already know, don't they? Am I always the last one to know everything?"

Beth had been working for Danvers International for about six months now as Suzy's assistant, ever since losing her job as an elementary school teacher due to budget cuts. Suzy handled event planning at Danvers and was engaged to Grayson Merimon, whom she had met a year ago when Danvers International merged with his company, Mericom, and created the largest communications company in the United States. They were both happy with the arrangement right now, and neither of them was ready to make a change.

She ran through her mind, trying to remember if Beth had been talking to anyone there more frequently than usual. "All right, I've got nothing. I'll give you credit, you can sneak around with the best of them because I'm totally clueless."

From Beth's expression, Suzy could tell she was debating the wisdom of revealing the father of her baby. Her options to force her to talk were limited, unfortunately. Since Beth had driven them, she would simply refuse to take Suzy home until she calmed down.

How much of a scene would she make in a restaurant? Beth wondered. *Just spit it out. I'm sure she will be happy. After all, you're keeping it in the family. She might be surprised, but she'll be happy for you. Just do it fast, like ripping off a Band-Aid.*

"Okay, um . . . It's Nick."

Suzy threw her head back and started laughing.

Wow, she sure was taking this well. Beth laughed along with her, relieved that Suzy didn't seem to be upset over her involvement with Nick.

Suzy wiped her eyes, still smiling. "Okay, sis, enough delaying. Spill the name already."

Oh, crap, I should have known it wasn't going to go that well. "Suzy, I'm serious, it's Nick. We've been seeing each other since we were both living with you after your accident. I mean, not immediately, but after a few weeks. It just happened. One minute I hated him and the next minute we were on the kitchen counter naked."

"Ugh, please stop! Tell me you're kidding? How can you possibly be sleeping with Nick? He's like our brother. That little shit. I should have known he couldn't be trusted to keep his pants on. He seduced you, didn't he?"

Beth grimaced as she took in her sister's glowing red face. "Suzy, I'm not a kid, and it's not his fault. Honestly, I practically ripped his clothes off."

Suzy was starting to feel light-headed. Why hadn't she suspected anything? Nick was around a lot. Where you saw Beth, he was normally close behind. Never once though had she thought anything of it. She had just been glad that they were getting along better. Ugh, she had forced them together at every turn, trying to keep the peace. *Oh, God, I'm her pimp. I have been setting my*

sister up for sex with my future brother-in-law. I've done
everything but pay the man to do my sister.

"Get your stuff; we're going back to my place. I want
to hear all about this, but I need to be drunk first."

"Bu— But Gray will be there."

"Does he know about this?"

"No, I promise you, he doesn't know anything. Ella
is the only other person who knows."

"Trust me, if Gray's home, he will make himself
scarce when he sees my face. Now, let's get out of here."

The silence in the car during the drive to Suzy's house
was broken only by an occasional groan from her. Beth
decided to stay quiet and let her come to terms with it
on the way. It wasn't like she was doing much better.
She still had a hard time believing that she was sleeping with someone like Nick. Never in her wildest
dreams could she have imagined a man like him being
interested in her. She had never been comfortable with
her body, even though she was a normal size now,
maybe even smaller than average for her height. Yet
when Nick looked at her, she felt beautiful. Even when
she tried to hide her body from him, he refused to let
her. He had kissed every inch of her, and the desire in
his eyes said that he didn't see any of the flaws that she
did. *Maybe he just needs glasses or he has secretly longed for*
a fluffy girl to cushion his hard contours.

Beth had no idea how Nick would react to the news
of her surprise pregnancy. Everything about their rela-

tionship was casual. They did spend almost every night together, but there was never any talk of feelings. For all she knew, he was still fitting in dates with other women when he could. She wasn't sure what her feelings were for him, either. If she let herself, she would probably fall madly in love with him. The only thing that stopped her was the certainty that men like Nick didn't end up with girls like her.

He was a rich, sexy, handsome man with a killer personality. Everyone loved him. When he walked into a room, it lit up with his presence. Things were just better when he was around. Beth, on the other hand, knew she was just average at best. Some might consider her attractive, but she was far from model material, and those were the kinds of women Nick was probably used to dating. She couldn't work out what he could possibly see in her besides maybe the excitement of sneaking around? *Boy, there had been plenty of that. They'd had hot, furious sex all over Suzy's new home.* Beth chuckled; her sister would croak if she knew that.

"All right, stop with the laughing. I can well imagine what's running through your mind, so please stop unless you want me to upchuck right here in your precious VW Bug."

Gray's BMW was sitting in the garage beside Suzy's SUV when they pulled in. "I'm not talking in front of him. So unless he goes, I go."

Suzy snorted and marched toward the door. "Trust me, I got this." When Suzy threw open the door to the beach house that she shared with her fiancé, she looked around as if moving in for the kill. When Gray picked that particular moment to walk in from the patio, Beth almost felt sorry for him. A smile lit up his face as he walked toward her sister, the love he felt for her evident in the intimate look in his eyes. As he leaned in for a kiss, Suzy put out a hand and stiff-armed him. "Whoooa, that's close enough, slick."

Any other man would be confused by such a statement, but Gray seemed to take it all in stride. "Good evening, Beth." When she smiled weakly at him, he turned back to Suzy. "Ah, baby, it would appear that I'm in the doghouse again. We could save time if you just tell me what I'm guilty of."

"You're guilty of having a horny brother who lowered his zipper in the wrong place this time!"

Beth could see the instant Gray looked at her and made the connection. "Oh, hell. I'll kill him," Gray sighed.

"You won't have to; I'm going to stick my foot so far up his ass, he may never walk right again."

Beth looked back and forth between her sister and Gray as they each threatened bodily harm to Nick in turn. This was really absurd. Nick hadn't seduced some teenager; she was an adult, fast approaching thirty. What did it say about her that they thought she was this easily led astray? *Poor fat Beth, she has to be protected from evil Nick. Show the big girl some attention and she loses her head.*

Screw this, she had had enough.

"Stop! My God, do you hear yourselves? Nick hasn't done anything wrong. Let me tell you—I wanted him. Hell, I still want him. I like sex; actually I love sex! Nick tried to be a gentleman and walk away after our first kiss, but you know what? I grabbed him and crammed my tongue down his throat and ripped the buttons off his shirt right in your kitchen. I have been fully willing and eager every time we have had sex and, believe me, we've had plenty. I'm enjoying myself and when I'm ready, I'll walk away."

When Beth paused to take a breath, she saw the stunned expressions on Suzy's and Gray's faces. Okay, possibly she might have gone a bit too far in her defense of Nick. Maybe a simple sentence letting them know it had been consensual would have been better than, "Hey, I'm a slut."

"Um, I think I'll go upstairs to my office. You know, take care of a few things. I'm sure you two would like some privacy." Gray left the room as fast as his Italian loafers would carry him.

Great, I'll never be able to look him in the eyes again. Every time he goes in his kitchen, he's going to imagine me ripping his brother's clothes off against his granite countertops.

Suzy pointed her to the couch in the living room before she walked into the kitchen. Moments later, she returned with a bottle of wine, orange juice, and two glasses. She motioned for Beth to be quiet until she had filled her glass to the rim and then proceeded to drain half of it. Taking a deep breath, she said, "All right, start at the beginning and feel free to gloss over any parts that you know will make me want to puke."

Beth picked up the glass of juice that Suzy had poured for her and took a sip while trying to decide where to begin. Well, heck, if she wanted the whole story, then that was what she would get.

Chapter Two

Six Months Earlier

Beth stood in the waiting room of the hospital with Claire and Jason. Her sister had been injured in an accident and Beth was waiting to see her. She was talking to Claire when a drop-dead gorgeous man strolled through the emergency room doors. Immediately the eyes of every woman—hers included—were riveted to him, or more specifically, to his butt. She was surprised when Jason said, "Hey, Nick, over here, man."

Mr. Hunk flashed a blinding smile that would do Colgate proud and swaggered over to where they were standing. He shook hands with Jason and then pulled Claire in for a hug. When those blue eyes landed on her, she had the urge to step behind the ficus tree beside her and try to blend into the scenery.

Jason stepped forward to make the introductions. "Beth, have you met Gray's brother, Nick?"

"Um, no, I haven't." She cringed as Nick extended his hand. He was so attractive she was almost hesitant to touch the man. Reluctantly, she placed her hand in his and was surprised to feel a bolt of heat race through her. She instinctively pulled her hand back quickly, making his eyebrows arch in question at her.

"Nice to meet you, Beth. I've heard only good things about your sister." She could feel her cheeks blushing furiously as he continued to study her.

Unable to bear his scrutiny another moment, Beth mumbled, "I'm going to see if they will let me back there to see her yet."

"Good idea, I'll walk with you," Nick offered.

Well, damn, that didn't work out at all. Not only am I still stuck with him, he's right on my heels where he can't help but see every lump in my oversized butt. Mr. Perfect probably hasn't seen this much wiggle since his last bowl of Jell-O. She walked to the nurses' station and was told that Suzy had been moved to a room. She had hoped Nick would at least wait in the waiting room or the hallway, but no such luck; he was practically stuck to her back as she opened the door to her sister's room.

Another hot specimen of manhood was sitting at Suzy's bedside holding her hand. This must be Gray. Why in the world was Suzy trying to get rid of him? The man was hot with a capital *H*! This whole situation was becoming something of a nightmare for Beth. She had never felt that comfortable around the opposite sex, even though she was working on that particular issue, but to be in such a small room with not one, but two of the hottest guys she had ever met, well, it felt like pure hell. She resisted the urge to start tugging at the long dress she wore. Was it riding up? Did her back look fat? Did she have granny-panty lines? The list of insecurities seemed to go on and on. These were men who would have you panting one second, and then praying to God that they would never see you naked the next.

Gray smiled at her and stepped forward to introduce himself. Yes, of course his dental work was just as exceptional as his brother's. What had she expected really, buckteeth? She was extremely grateful when he stepped outside the room with his brother and left her alone with Suzy. *I can really see why you would want to get away from that, sis. I mean, the man is just gross. His hair is too perfect and that body, I just hate it when men don't let themselves go. Where are his love handles? His five-hundred dollar cologne is sickeningly seductive and that butt, ugh, please. Run while you can, the man is a toad.*

Gray walked back into the room at that moment and she was relieved to see that Nick wasn't with him. After she made arrangements with Gray to come back the following morning, he insisted on walking her out to her car. Ugh, was she going to spend the rest of the evening with the Merimons trailing her down a hallway? When they reached her little red VW Bug, she found herself asking him about Nick. She wanted to clamp her hand over her mouth as soon as his name came out and she could see the surprise and possibly concern in Gray's eyes. When he told her that Nick was also going to be moving to Myrtle Beach, she felt her heart skip a beat. What was wrong with her? He was way out of her league. Maybe it was just wishful lusting.

After Suzy was released from the hospital, Beth was a frequent visitor to Gray's home where Suzy was to stay while she recovered. Suzy had a broken ankle and, since both Suzy and Beth lived on the upper floors of their buildings, Gray had insisted they stay with him. He wanted to keep Suzy close so he could monitor her recovery, and he invited Beth to make herself at home there as well, so she could help keep an eye on Suzy. At Gray's beautiful beachfront home, she ran into Nick daily and he always had some remark to make. He had taken to calling her "princess" and she felt sure that he was only doing it to mock her. No matter how she snapped at him, it never seemed to hit the mark. He just laughed it off and an hour later he was back to picking on her again. She alternated between drooling over his hard body and wanting to strangle him with the kitchen towel.

Was she imagining the sexual tension that seemed to vibrate between them? Surely, it was only on her part. It had been a long time since she had been with anyone that didn't require batteries. Maybe it was time to go home, pop open the toy drawer, and release some tension.

Who would ever believe that the poor spinster sister

would have one toy, much less a couple? Suzy would fall over in a dead faint if she found out. Not that Beth had any intention of ever talking about sexy toys with her sister. Of course, Suzy would probably be proud of her and present her with a coupon from somewhere like Vibrators-R-Us. Just because she wasn't having sex didn't mean she wouldn't like to. Weren't women supposed to be in their sexual prime around thirty? If that were true, it might be time to stock a case of Duracells for these hard times.

Before Beth really understood what was happening between them, she had suddenly started changing the way she dressed. She couldn't bear for Nick to see her in her frumpy wear. She tried to tell herself it was just so she wouldn't embarrass Suzy at the office, but a part of her knew it was so that Nick would look at her with something other than laughter for once.

One evening they had decided to have a barbecue at the beach house and invite their friends from Danvers. Claire, Jason, Ella, and Declan Stone, the new guy to their group, all attended that night. She had sat beside Nick at the patio table while they had dinner. She was wearing a sundress, a sexy red thong, and a matching bra that she had purchased at Victoria's Secret that day on a whim. She had to admit that she was feeling just a little naughty with such sexy undergarments. She was usually more of a Sears catalogue type of gal. Nick was wearing a pair of cargo shorts, so every time either of them shifted, their bare legs came into contact. After a while, she was starting to wonder if Nick was making sure that happened a lot more often than it should have.

By the time everyone left for the evening, she was feeling pretty hot and bothered. Had Nick missed a single opportunity to touch her during dinner? No doubt he thought it was pretty funny. Let's feel the fat girl up and give her the thrill of her life. Sadly, it probably *was* one of Beth's bigger thrills, at least in recent history. She was more than a little pissed at him when she stomped into the kitchen with the last of the dinner plates. When she saw him leaning against the counter drinking a beer, she wanted to stomp her feet and throw an honest-to-goodness tantrum. Couldn't she go anywhere that he wasn't in her face?

Nick's mouth curved into a slow grin as he looked at her. "Hey, princess, need some help with that?"

"No, I've got it," Beth snapped. She walked over, dropped the dishes loudly onto the counter beside the dishwasher, and started stacking them inside.

"What's the problem, princess?"

Beth slammed the last plate in the dishwasher and whirled around to confront him. He looked wary as she opened her mouth to blast him. To both of their surprise, instead of the tirade she had planned, she grabbed the front of his shirt and pulled him down to her while she raised herself on her toes. Just before she locked her mouth onto his, he whispered, "Princess?"

Nick put down his beer with a sexy groan and

wrapped his arms around her. Suddenly, his mouth took control of the kiss and his tongue entered her mouth as if he wanted to possess her. She moaned low in her throat, as he grabbed her butt cheeks to pull her closer. She had no idea how long they stood there, but she did know that she had never been kissed as Nick was kissing her. He sucked on her tongue, as if he couldn't get enough. Every stroke, every sip only made her burn hotter. He rocked his hips against hers in tempo with his tongue tangling with hers. Beth could feel him hard against her stomach and she wantonly rubbed against his length and felt a heady sense of power when he rumbled deep in his throat.

Abruptly, he lifted his head and pulled away from her, staggering backward as if drunk. He leaned against the counter, running a shaky hand through his hair. "Ah, hell, we can't do this, princess. Your sister and my brother will kill me. My God, you taste so good though. Shit!"

Beth looked at him and for once decided to break all the rules. Tonight she wouldn't be denied—the good girl was going bad and it was time for Nick to live up to his reputation. She smiled and gave him a predatory look as she stalked forward. His eyes were riveted to hers as she reached for the hem of his button-down shirt. With a mighty yank, buttons flew all over the kitchen and Nick's mouthwatering chest was laid naked before her hungry eyes. *That wouldn't have been nearly as hot if those buttons hadn't given way. Thank God for poor sewing!*

Nick's eyes were nearly bugging out of the sockets by this point. "Fuck, Beth; screw it! I tried to be good, but I have got to have you now—I can't stop again."

With those words, Nick reached down and grabbed the bottom of her dress, pulling it up and over her head in one smooth move. She stood before him in her sandals, thong, and demi-bra. She had never been so thankful for a good set of underwear. "My God, princess, you're beautiful. You have been driving me out of my mind and that was before I knew what was under your clothes."

A sense of urgency took over and Beth knew this wouldn't be a slow lovemaking. This was going to be hot, sweaty sex and that was just the way she wanted it. Nick reached out and palmed her breasts through her bra, quickly working the nipples to stiff peaks before sliding his hand down her stomach and cupping her sex in his hand. She knew he could feel the moisture through the thin silk material as he rubbed her into a frenzy.

In a move that would have put a stripper to shame, he had her bra and panties off as well his remaining clothes. She grimaced as he swung her effortlessly up and sat her on the counter. "Condom, we need a condom," he managed to gasp out.

"No, I'm on the pill, we're fine," Beth moaned, impatient now for his possession. Nick looked like he had just received his birthday present early as he gave her that sexy grin. She reached forward to take his impressive length into her hand. She circled her finger around his tip, rubbing in the moisture that was gathering there.

Nick groaned. "Princess, you better let that go if you want this to last more than a minute." He gently removed her hands from his cock and pushed her back until she was lying on the counter with her hips almost hanging off the edge.

She felt his tip nudging against her slick entrance and shivers raced up and down her body. *My God, I'm really doing this. I'm going to have sex with Nick Freaking Merimon right now and I could come just thinking about it.*

Nick remained poised at her entrance, seeming transfixed by the sight of the bodies touching so intimately. His breathing was ragged as he trailed an unsteady hand down her neck and then circled each nipple. He then moved his caresses lower and lightly brushed against her damp curls, seeking the place where his cock rested against her slick opening. "God, you're so beautiful and you look like pure sex lying open to me like this."

When his finger slid over her clit, Beth almost came up off the counter. She wrapped her legs around his hips, trying to pull him forward into the place inside her that was desperate for his possession.

"You want that, baby?" Nick moaned. "Then take it, take what you need!"

Beth didn't need any further urging; she wrapped her legs tighter and pumped her hips forward, driving him deep into her. Her inner muscles quivered as he filled her almost to the point of pain. She knew that she should give her body a chance to get used to his invasion, but she was powerless to stop. Desire like she had never known was ripping through her, and her only focus was on ending the relentless ache that throbbed through her body. She pumped her hips against him harder, forcing him in to the hilt and then continued to grind herself against him, trying to take him even deeper.

Nick growled in his throat almost like an animal and suddenly his thrusts were meeting hers. He seemed no longer content to let her take the lead. He left little doubt as to who was in control as he took her ankles from behind his hips and lifted them up over his shoulders. He slid in so deep that Beth felt him rubbing against her cervix. He gripped her hips tightly in his hands and held her in place on the counter while he pounded into her. The kitchen was filled with the sounds of their moans and heavy breathing as they both raced toward their peak.

Beth felt herself starting to quiver as the first ripples of her orgasm started. "Nick, oh myyyy Goddd, Nick, don't stop!" As pleasure started to tear through her in waves, Nick reached out to roughly flick her clit and she exploded. Her orgasm went on and on as he continued to pound into her. Just when she thought it wasn't possible, she felt herself start to crest another orgasm as Nick rammed into her. He stiffened with a shout as he reached his own climax.

Beth thought she would pass out from the sensations running through her body. Nick released her legs and fell forward, almost toppling them both off the counter. His head landed against her stomach and she felt his sweat pooling in her navel. She idly ran her hands through his damp hair, enjoying this moment of closeness before she severed it.

"Shit, princess, you damn near killed me." Nick chuckled. "You are a damn tiger under that innocent, schoolteacher exterior, aren't you?"

Beth smiled, pleased that she could bring a playboy like Nick literally to his knees. Apparently, those self-help books were really paying off. What she lacked in experience she more than made up for in research.

Ruffling his hair one last time, Beth said, "Help me down, Romeo. I have a bag of bagels wedged under my head."

Beth almost groaned as Nick slowly slid out of her, causing a delicious friction every inch of the way. One look into his face and she knew it was intentional. "You're a bad boy, Nick, you really are." When she finally had her feet on the floor, she deliberately stretched her body like a cat, working out all of the kinks that sex on the hard counter had caused. She noticed on the last stretch that she had Nick's full attention visually and physically.

As he reached for her, she sidestepped his arms and started to gather her clothes. When she looked up at him, he had a puzzled expression on his handsome face. No doubt, he was used to women hanging all over him postcoital. She patted one of his firm butt cheeks on the way out the kitchen door and smiled to herself at the stunned expression on his face.

The sound of Suzy gagging beside her brought Beth back to the present. Suzy took a huge gulp of wine and groaned. "My god, Beth, I told you I didn't need all of the details. How am I supposed to look Quick-Zipper in the eyes again knowing what he did to you on *my* counter?"

Beth laughed as she said, "I believe the better question here, sis, is how will you look him in the eyes knowing what I did to him on your counter? Every time we have sex, he seems to expect something more. Why can't he just accept that I want to have sex with him without being his girlfriend?"

"Well, I don't know; maybe because you are pregnant with his child?" Suzy snapped.

Beth waved her off. "No, that's not it. He doesn't know about that yet. It's not a game changer anyway. I still don't plan to get involved with him. Nick is a player and that might make him really, really, *really* great in bed, but it doesn't make him a good father figure. He can be involved, but I will be the parent to my child."

Suzy looked at her as if stunned. "Just who in the hell are you, Beth? You know I'm far from a prude, but I have to say I hardly recognize you. It's not that I'm putting down your choices, because I'm the last person who should throw stones, but you just seem so different from the person I always thought you to be. It's blowing my damn mind into a million pieces. I'm horrified and strangely proud of you all at the same time. Nick really didn't take advantage of you, did he?"

With a smile of supreme satisfaction, Beth said, "Nope, he had very little say in the matter. Don't get me wrong, I don't sleep around. You know I haven't slept with many guys. And Nick is the first man I have had sex with in years." Then, almost embarrassed to admit it, she continued, "I wanted him though, sis, and for once I didn't let the fat me talk me out of it. I know we are nothing alike and it's not going to go anywhere. I won't let him break my heart, but I'm enjoying the ride."

"Shit on a stick, Beth! Hellllooo! This just went from sowing some delayed wild oats to a serious, life-altering complication. You do realize that your life has changed forever, don't you?" Suzy asked more gently.

Smiling, Beth said, "Yeah, I do and I couldn't be happier. I've always wanted to have a family and finally I get what I want. It might not be the fairy-tale version, but it's closer than I ever imagined."

"Can I ask you something else? Why are you talking about Nick as if you already know he won't be sticking around? Are you sure he doesn't know?"

"Nope, he is totally clueless."

"I can't believe I'm saying this," Suzy groaned, "but

you should give the guy a chance to do the right thing. I know he has probably given more rides than Greyhound, but deep down he seems like a good guy."

After all of these years, Suzy never failed to surprise her with some of the things that came out of her mouth. Comparing Nick to the Greyhound bus line? She idly wondered how Suzy would react to knowing that even though she hadn't slept with many men, she had been on a bit of a dating marathon the last few months. Somehow, she didn't think Suzy was ready to deal with any more information tonight. Her bottle of wine was long since empty and her sister still looked shell-shocked.

But after another moment of deep thought, Suzy said, "So this has been going on for a while. How in the world have you managed to keep it hidden?"

Beth laughed. "It's been rather easy. No one suspects the fat girl of screwing the hot guy's brains out. I could have been doing him in the office when you walked in and your mind would have come up with some other way to justify it. I'm just not hot-guy material."

"Damn it, Beth, you are not a fat girl! Why must you continue to harp on that? The only reason I wouldn't have suspected you two of sleeping with each other is because you and Nick are always arguing. Ugh, now I know that's just foreplay. You're a beautiful woman, and I have no doubt that Nick had a boner every time you walked past."

Chuckling, Beth said, "Wow, when did you become

such a romantic? Settling down with Gray has done wonders for you. I can only imagine how you sweet talk him."

With a feline smile, Suzy said, "Trust me, Gray has no complaints about anything concerning my mouth."

"Oh, gross! Please don't go there; leave me with some of my ignorance."

"What are you bitching about? I'm the one who is going to have to tear the damned counters out of my kitchen because I'll never be able to use them again without wondering if your butt cheek was on that section."

"Touché, sis. You've got me there," Beth agreed.

"When do you plan to tell Nick about the baby?"

"Well, obviously before it's born." When Suzy elbowed her, Beth sighed. "Probably tonight. He's supposed to come over this evening, so after we, um, well you know, then I'll see if I have the energy to tell him."

Luckily, she was saved from Suzy's comment when Gray walked hesitantly into the room. He looked as if he was prepared to dive for cover at any moment.

Beth took pity on him. "It's okay, Gray. I'm getting ready to leave." She took advantage of the distraction that Gray offered and quickly grabbed her purse. She gave Suzy a fast hug and smiled at Gray as he insisted on walking her to her car.

He reached for her door handle, but instead of opening it, he turned to look at her. "Beth, are you okay?" he asked quietly.

She was touched to see the look of concern in his eyes. Suzy had hit the jackpot when she met Gray, and a part of Beth couldn't help but feel a little envious. She might be sleeping with a Merimon brother, but he was as different as night from day from Gray. Smiling reassuringly at him, she said, "I'm fine, Gray, really I am. I hope Suzy doesn't give you a hard time about Nick. He isn't the bad guy in all of this. If anyone is, it's me."

Beth could see that she had surprised Gray yet again. He gave her a shrewd look and said, "Be careful, Beth. Whether you mean to or not, you're giving my brother something that he won't be able to resist: a challenge. I doubt he has ever had a woman walk away."

"I don't know what you mean. Both Nick and I know where things stand between us. I bet he's blowing the dust off his little black book as we speak."

With a tired sigh, Gray said, "All right, but don't say I didn't warn you." He leaned over to kiss her cheek and then opened the door for her. "Be careful driving home and, um, tell my brother I said hello."

Chapter Three

Suzy laid her head back on the couch, trying to come to terms with everything she'd learned from her conversation with Beth. Apparently, the quiet ones were always hiding something. She almost felt sorry for Nick. She was fairly certain that her sister had seduced him right out of his pants. This whole thing might be kind of funny if not for the baby.

She opened her eyes to see Gray standing in front of her, visibly braced for her assault. She held her hand out to him, suddenly more thankful than ever to have such a wonderful man in her life. He took her hand and settled in beside her. She laid her head against his chest and snuggled back into his arms.

"What's going on, baby?" Gray asked quietly.

With a sigh, Suzy said, "Beth's pregnant and Nick's the father."

She felt Gray stiffen against her. This was all hitting too close to home for them. Just months ago, their relationship had almost been destroyed by a woman from Gray's past claiming to be pregnant with his child. If not for Reva's sudden attack of conscience, they may well have lost each other. She knew that it was a hard blow to Gray, but she also knew that he would support his brother and Beth no matter what.

"Ah, shit. Does my brother know?"

"No, I think she's going to tell him tonight. God, Gray, how could I have been so blind? I never suspected anything was going on between them. I was so desperate for them to stop arguing that I even pushed them together at every turn. I might as well have bought them a set of handcuffs and some Cool Whip. I practically made this happen."

With a chuckle Gray said, "Well, I don't know about the handcuffs, but a box of condoms might have come in handy."

Suzy smacked his chest, but couldn't help the laugh that escaped her lips. "Well, if I had thought my sister was getting busy with someone, you bet I would have covered that base. It wasn't Nick, though. Apparently, he tried to be good for once. I never thought I'd be saying this but supposedly my sister seduced your brother. The only person who can drop Nick's zipper faster than him seems to be Beth."

"Wow," Gray murmured. "I just never imagined Beth . . . I mean, um . . . wow."

Groaning, Suzy said, "Yeah, I know exactly what you mean. I don't even know how to process this. Things were much easier when I thought my sister was the innocent little wallflower seduced by your gigolo brother. At least then I would have a clear course of action. Kick his ass and then help her pick up the pieces. Now I'm in the uncomfortable position of feeling like I need to protect Nick from my cougar sister."

Gray gave her shoulders a squeeze and laughed. "Trust me, baby, my brother has never been innocent a day in his life, so don't make him the saint here. He might have been swayed the first time, but unless Beth had him chained up somewhere, he's been sleeping with her all this time of his own free will."

Suzy turned and wrapped herself around Gray. When his lips settled onto hers, she felt the world slip away, as it always did whenever he touched her.

Beth smiled as she pulled into her parking space in front of her apartment and saw Nick's Audi in her other space. For weeks he had been driving a minivan that he had rented while his car was in the shop. The van really had come in handy while Suzy was on crutches with a broken ankle. The three of them had gotten rather attached to it and, even though he wouldn't admit it, she thought Nick had been a little sad to see it go as well. The Audi R8 definitely suited him more though—a two-door sports car that he adored. Beth had to admit, she felt a bit like a bad girl when she rode in it. It might not be sensible, but man was it sexy.

As she stepped in front of her door on the second floor, it suddenly flung open. "God, Beth, where have you been? You got off work hours ago. I called you several times and no answer. I was afraid something had happened to you."

Beth was surprised to see Nick visibly disheveled. "Um, sorry, you knew I was meeting Suzy for a drink after work."

"That was hours ago. Where the hell did you go for a drink, Atlanta? I called you, Suzy, and Gray. Have you all stopped answering your damn phones?"

Good grief, what had gotten into him? Sure, she was a little later than usual, but she hadn't thought he would notice, much less be upset about it. Walking over to him, she went up on her tiptoes and wrapped her arms around his neck. She felt the familiar desire start to hum through her body as she looked at his handsome features. Nick Merimon was every woman's wet dream. He made her heart pound and her body go slick with need in an instant. He turned her into a wanton, intent only on having his body any way she could.

With Nick, she could pretend that she was someone else. There was freedom with him because he never knew "fat Beth." She didn't think she could ever be comfortable dating—much less sleeping with—anyone who knew her when she was heavier. In her mind, they would be turned off by who she used to be. She felt like someone other than that plain, overweight girl she'd always been when she was with Nick. In his eyes, she was pretty and sexy and that is exactly how she felt with him.

Beth had come to the realization a while back that in order to find someone to spend her life with, she would have to date outside her circle and, boy, had she been. Things had gotten complicated when she became involved with Nick and suddenly her two worlds were colliding.

The feel of Nick's warm mouth against the side of her neck had her nipples suddenly standing at attention. God, did that man know how to use his tongue. Outside the impressive package between his legs, that had become her favorite part of him. *When did I turn into such a guy? Shouldn't I be concerned about his feelings or love him for his mind or at least his sense of humor? Instead, I just lust after his body. I'm a T and A girl now. Well, tongue and ass that is.*

Between nips to her lower lip, Nick growled, "I missed you today, princess."

Beth smiled at him. She knew this was a part of his whole seduction routine. If she ever let herself believe that she was special to him, then she was finished. Nick was an all-around good guy and he really loved women. He not only wanted you to feel special while making love, he wanted you to feel special before and after. It was probably why women seemed to love him even when he was showing them the door. It was one of the things she respected about him. He would go a mile out of his way to keep from hurting someone's feelings, especially a woman's feelings.

He slid his hands from her waist to the bottom of her

dress, bunching it up in his hands. Pulling it up her body, he moaned low in his throat when he brushed his hand against her bare bottom. "The thong was the single best invention of this century. I hope you aren't attached to this, princess."

Before she could answer, Nick snapped the fragile lace on one side and let it slide down her legs. When it reached her ankles, she kicked it off. Without releasing her, he quickly lowered the shorts he was wearing and kicked them away. He lifted her off her feet and she automatically wrapped her legs around his waist. He backed her up against the wall and her breath left her lungs on a whoosh as he impaled her on his cock.

Beth's neck arched back as she moaned in pleasure. He held her hips, setting a relentless pace as his body pumped into hers. Her body recognized his from the first stroke. The emptiness she felt when they were apart was only ever truly filled when his body was joined with hers. She tried hard not to think about what would happen when he was no longer there to take that ache away.

Sweat rolled from their bodies and Nick continued to claim every inch of her. His tongue licked her neck and then took possession of her mouth. She moaned at the taste of him. She could spend hours a day twirling her tongue with his. As her body started to tighten, she ground her hips against his, desperate for a release from the tension that threatened to split her apart.

As if sensing that she was close to the edge, Nick

started swiveling his hips causing his cock to rub against her clit. The sensation was exquisite as pleasure radiated out from the sensitive nub. With another hard thrust, Beth exploded. The tremors shaking her body sent Nick to his own orgasm and, with a shout, he emptied himself inside her.

Still joined with her, he staggered to a chair. She collapsed against his chest, too tired to move. Sitting in the chair with her legs still wrapped around Nick and his cock still nestled inside her was one of the most intimate moments of her life. She felt his lips brush against her forehead as one last shudder shook his body.

"I guess you're forgiven for being late, princess. Wall sex is gonna make me forgive and forget most every time."

Beth chuckled. "I'll keep that in mind. Ugh, I need a shower, but I don't have the energy to get there."

"Just hold on, baby, I'll get us there."

Beth sighed with regret as he gently pulled out of her and then tried to protest as he lifted her and walked through the bedroom to the bathroom. She was flattered to see that he didn't look winded by the trip.

The shower was a quick affair. Both of them were too tired to attempt anything other than washing. They were already snuggled under the bedcover when she remembered that she had decided to tell him her news tonight. With a yawn, she decided it could wait until tomorrow and she drifted off.

*   *   *

Something woke Beth from a sound sleep. She lay there for a moment, disoriented until a crushing wave of sickness rolled over her. Pressing a hand to her mouth, she stumbled from the bed, almost sprinting to the bathroom. She barely got the lid up on the toilet before she emptied her stomach of its contents. As she sat on the floor wondering if there was going to be another round, she heard Nick knock on the door.

"Princess, are you okay?"

Before she could answer, round two was well on its way and she was again hanging over the toilet, even though there appeared to be nothing left. She felt Nick's hand on her back and then he was pulling her hair back from the line of fire. After a few moments, she was down to nothing but dry heaves so she dropped to the floor and sat back against the bathroom cabinet. Nick grabbed a cloth and wet it under the faucet before gently cleaning her face. She felt the strange urge to start crying when she looked into his concern-filled eyes.

"Honey, are you all right?"

Beth nodded, too weak to say the words. Nick finished cleaning her up and then left the room. He came back a few moments later with a fresh gown and, without saying a word, he pulled her to her feet and used one arm to support her while using the other to strip the now soiled gown off and put the clean one on. He helped her brush her teeth and rinse her mouth and then he leaned down and hooked his arms under her knees, lifting her in his arms. Had she not been so weak she would have been horrified at him carrying her, but now she was just grateful for the help.

He had pulled the covers back on her side and now he sat her down and grabbed some extra pillows to prop up her head. When he had her tucked in to his satisfaction, he sat down beside her and gently brushed her hair out of her face. "Better now?" he asked.

"Oh, yes, thank you, Nick," she rasped out.

"What happened, princess? Was it something you ate last night?"

Damn, the stupid tears were back in her eyes. What was wrong with her tonight? Had throwing up always made her an emotional wreck? *Tell him, just get it over with.* Beth opened her mouth to do just that and found no sound coming out at all. No matter how hard she tried, the words would not come. *Chickenshit, you have to tell him.*

Nick gave her a sweet kiss on the forehead and went to get her a bottle of water. Her eyes were getting heavier by the moment, and when he returned, she was already asleep.

Chapter Four

Despite Nick's protests, Beth made it into the head-quarters of Danvers International only a few minutes late for work. She took a deep breath and then tapped on her sister's door. Smiling at the grunt she heard in response, she opened the door and walked in. Suzy would never be a morning person and even living with Gray hadn't changed that. On those mornings when she did come in unusually perky, Beth knew exactly why. Gray brought out the soft side in her and Beth had never seen her happier. With a small sigh, Beth hoped she'd have a love like that someday.

Suzy turned a sharp gaze on her as if expecting some type of war wounds. "So, what did he say? Are you going to make me beg?"

Beth dropped in the chair in front of her desk and braced herself. "I haven't told him yet."

"What! Why the hell not? I thought you were going to take care of that last night."

Shifting in her seat, Beth murmured, "Um, something came up."

"What do you mean, something came up?" Suzy demanded.

Beth could feel the blush starting to work its way up her neck and into her face. It was too much to hope that Suzy wouldn't notice.

"Oh, yuck! God, Beth, isn't that how this happened to start with? Can't you two keep your clothes on for more than five minutes?"

With a wiggle of her eyebrows, Beth purred, "Trust me, I remember exactly how this happened."

"All right, just please stop. I already had to take the stairs this morning when I saw Nick getting on the elevator. Do you have any idea how many damn stairs I had to climb because you can't keep your hands off the guy? You owe me a new pair of shoes and a pedicure."

Beth tried hard, but she couldn't contain the laughter that bubbled out when she thought of Suzy climbing all of those flights of stairs just to avoid Nick. The only person who hated exercise more than Beth was her sister. "I almost told him this morning, after I threw my guts up. I think I had my first bout of morning sickness."

Suzy looked more closely at her with concern evident in her gaze. "Are you okay? Why did you come in today? Get your stuff and go back home, you shouldn't be here sick."

Holding up her hand to stop the onslaught, Beth assured her that she felt fine now. "I passed out in the bed before I could tell him. I'm going to talk to him tonight.

I'll have plenty of time to get my nerve up because we're just planning a quiet evening at home."

"Yeah, good, but if he says anything even remotely bad to you, call me and I'll be right over. I don't care who, um, instigated this, he still had to . . . you know. Ah, hell, he still shot the load without protection, so he is just as much to blame."

"Shot the load?" Beth groaned. "It's called sex, Suzy, and you know plenty about it since you live with Mr. Sex-on-a-Stick as you called him once."

Waving her toward the door, Suzy said, "Just go and don't come back for a while. Like maybe for the whole day while I try to scrub my mind of this entire conversation."

Beth chuckled and walked to her office. As she dropped her purse on her desk, her door suddenly shut behind her and warm hands slid around her waist. "Are you feeling better, princess?"

She smiled as she heard the sexy voice whispering in her ear. Allowing herself to snuggle back in his embrace for just a moment, she said, "Yeah, I'm fine now. What are you doing down here so early?"

Nick turned her around in his arms so they were facing each other. "I just wanted to make sure you were okay." He trailed a finger down the curve of her cheek and placed a kiss on the corner of her mouth. "I was worried about you. You were so sick this morning."

It was so hard to hold out against his charms, especially when he was in this kind of loving, gentle mood.

Keep it casual. He probably has the same routine with every woman he dates. He doesn't love you or even want to love you. He is just a nice guy. She gave him a quick smile and stepped out of the circle of his arms. "I'm fine, Nick, really. I feel great now." Walking around her desk to put some distance between them, she asked, "Are we still having dinner at my place tonight?"

Nick frowned, obviously confused about the distance that she tried to keep between them unless they were having sex. "Yeah, sure."

Beth started thumbing through a stack of papers on her desk, hoping that Nick would get the message and leave before she gave in to the urge to shove him down on her desk and ride that fabulous body.

As he started toward the door he suddenly turned around and asked, "What's up with Suzy? Just as I got on the elevator this morning I saw her walk up and then take off like a bat out of hell when she saw me standing there."

Beth quickly looked down, afraid her face would give her away. "Um, you know Suzy, it could have been anything. She probably never saw you."

Still looking doubtful, Nick said, "I guess you're right. I'll see you later on."

She flopped in her chair as the door shut behind him. Was it too early to be having pregnancy hormones? It was getting harder and harder not to buy into the idea of a relationship with him. But she knew that it would destroy her when he walked away and she couldn't risk it. Of course, now thanks to the baby, their lives would always be intertwined. With a sick feeling, she wondered how she would ever live through the many women she would be forced to see move in and out of his life. In the very near future, if he decided to be a father to their child, he could well have some other woman with him when he picked up their baby for a visit. A wave of nausea swept her, and she knew in her heart that this time it had very little to do with morning sickness.

Nick slowly shut Beth's door and walked down the hall. After sleeping with her for months, he didn't feel any closer to her than their first time on Gray's kitchen counter. Everyone assumed that he just jumped from one bed to another, but he seldom did that and the few times it had happened, he had hardly been proud of it.

He had never planned on getting involved with Beth, even though she had intrigued him from their first meeting. Her obvious dislike of him was like fuel on a fire. The more she rolled her eyes at him, the more he teased her. She hated him calling her *princess* so he made sure he did it regularly. What had started as an innocent game had fast gotten out of control. He found himself making up reasons to stay at Gray's with Beth and Suzy while she was injured. He shuffled his schedule and worked far into the night so that he could free up more time to help. Of course, he would have done anything that Suzy needed and he knew that Gray was grateful that he was staying there while he was away. Truthfully, though, he just couldn't seem to stay away from Beth.

He was an affectionate person by nature and he usually had some level of closeness with the women he was involved with. Admittedly, it might be a brief relationship, but he still cared, to some degree, even after it was over. He couldn't understand why Beth seemed so determined to keep him at arm's length.

She'd given him more than one hard-on before they'd finally had sex. Probably the most memorable one was in Victoria's Secret when Suzy dragged them there to shop for something for Gray's return home after a long business trip. Nick had started by playfully holding up skimpy bra and panty sets trying to embarrass Beth. She finally walked off, clearly pissed off. He'd let her go, giving her time to fume in private. As he was wandering around the store waiting for them both to be finished, he spotted Beth holding a pair of lacy black thong panties. Just when he felt sweat starting to break out on his forehead, she grabbed what looked to be a dozen pairs of them in various colors and matching lacy bras.

He had felt his erection starting to dig painfully into the zipper of his jeans when she paused at the end of the aisle and picked up a garter belt. She acted as if she wore stuff like that every day. He stood rooted in the same spot for at least five minutes trying to get control of his body. He really didn't want to be the weird pervert that went into a lingerie store to get his thrills. Luckily, he had gotten himself under control by the time he saw the girls paying for their purchases. Every time he saw that damn bag for the rest of the afternoon, he felt his cock stirring. He was practically saying "Down, boy" every few minutes.

The night they'd finally had sex had blown him away. He wanted her so much by then that he was constantly on pins and needles when she was near. Her scent when she walked by drove him crazy. She smelled like a citrus mixture of exotic fruit and flowers. He actually caught himself sniffing when she left the room, hoping for a whiff of that enticing scent.

He had been determined not to hit on her, though. He knew Suzy and Gray would kill him if he slept with her and, even though he longed to land in bed with her, he never did anything other than tease her. When they were cleaning up after a cookout at Gray's home, she had walked into the kitchen with the last of the dishes. He had started to tease her when she dropped the dishes loudly into the sink. He would never forget the look on her face. Her eyes narrowed at him as if in anger, but her cheeks were flushed and she was breathing as if she had just run a marathon.

Suddenly, she had gripped his shirt, pulling him down to her and slammed her mouth against his. Shock had rippled through his body for a split second before desire took over. His arms came around her and it was the hottest moment of his life. He had tried to step back at some point and give her a chance to walk away, but she had held on for dear life and he was too far gone to walk away from her again.

He had lost himself in her from that moment. Seeing her in a pair of those sexy little panties that she had purchased from Victoria's Secret had finished punching his ticket. There was no way he could have left that kitchen without having her. She was just as desperate for him as he was for her. He had never been with a woman so responsive. She knew exactly where he wanted to be stroked. She touched him like someone with a wealth of experience, yet when he entered her body, she was almost like a virgin, so small and tight. He almost lost it on the first stroke into her body and just barely managed to hold it together until he felt her orgasm. Such loss of control was foreign to him. He prided himself on his "ladies-first policy," but, boy, had he come close to violating it.

He was so blown away afterward that he just wanted to find a bed and curl himself around her lush body. Instead, she had essentially patted him on the head and walked away. *Say what?* Wasn't that supposed to be his exit move? Her bedroom door had closed firmly and that had been it. If he hadn't been so damned exhausted he would have trailed her into her room and insisted that she talk about what had just happened. *Since when did a guy have great sex with no strings and then want to dissect it all night long? She handed you every man's wet dream and you want to make it complicated?* And that was when he realized he was in over his head with her.

The next morning, Beth had acted as if nothing unusual had happened between them. No eye contact, no hot looks or seductive body language, nothing. By the time he left work that evening he was wondering if he had imagined the whole thing. He had almost convinced himself of that fact when he got in the elevator for the penthouse at Danvers where he was staying until he found something to purchase. He reached over to put his key card in when someone stepped onto the elevator. The polite smile froze on his face when he saw it was Beth.

Fire blazed in her eyes as her gaze locked on his. He tried to pull it together and have some semblance of cool, but it was all over when she lined her body up flush with his and pressed her soft curves against the hard lines of his body. He sucked in a ragged breath groaning, "Princess, what are you doing?"

A husky laugh escaped from her throat when she purred, "I'm doing you, Nick, that's what I'm doing." With those words, she had hooked her arms around his neck and drew his mouth to hers. Just as their tongues met and tangled, he heard the elevator chime for his floor. He backed her out the door, knowing there were probably cameras in the elevators and he didn't want to give security any added entertainment.

As he tried to fit his key in the door lock, Beth wrapped herself around his back and her hand wandered around to his front, lightly stroking against the growing bulge in his pants. He thought he would break the damn key trying to get the door open. The key suddenly turned and they fell inside when the door opened. They ripped each other's clothes off and Nick pulled Beth onto his lap on the couch. They both moaned as he slid inside of her.

That was how most of their sex life seemed to go. A frantic twist of hands, tongues, and bodies coming together as they raced to the finish line. He tried to slow it down. He wanted to spend an evening doing nothing but exploring her body. But Beth wouldn't allow slow and gentle. Whenever he tried, she did everything she could to drive him over the deep end until they ended fast and furious.

Damned if he could understand it. Not that he was complaining because, quite frankly, sex with her was mind-blowing. He just wished that sometimes she would let him slow the frantic pace. Not every time had to be a trip to the Indy 500.

He had no idea what he wanted from Beth, but he was tired of her treating him like a fuck buddy. *Go ahead and turn your guy card in because no man should complain about having hot sex with a beautiful woman whenever she wanted it.* Still, her attitude toward spending more time together bothered him. Maybe it was time to stop being so available. Tonight he would do what assholes all over the world did daily. He would stand her up for dinner and, for once, let her wonder where her Mr. Available was. Sitting around glued to her side wasn't getting him anywhere so maybe it was time to change things up.

Chapter Five

Where was Nick? Beth looked at her watch yet again and saw it was now after ten. He should have been here no later than six. Dinner had long since grown cold, but she'd left everything on the table, too pissed off to clean up. She had planned on telling the big jerk about the pregnancy tonight, but now all she wanted to do was yell and scream at him—and, God help her, she also wanted to sit down and cry.

For someone who claimed to want nothing from Nick, you certainly are overreacting at being stood up. With a groan of disgust, she went to the bedroom to get ready for bed. Already she seemed to tire much more easily than she normally did.

She awoke with a jolt. The room was spinning and her stomach was churning. She jumped out of bed and dove for the bathroom, where she once again lost the contents of her stomach. Since she had barely eaten anything earlier, it ended up being a lot of dry heaving after the initial sickness.

She was lying on the bathroom floor, too tired and

weak to make it back to bed, when she heard someone stumbling around in the bedroom. She heard a crash and a loud curse. She relaxed, recognizing Nick's voice. He knocked on the bathroom door and slurred a loud, "Princess, you in there?"

Before she could answer, the door burst open and Nick blinked several times while his eyes tried to adjust to the bright light. "What're you doing on the floor, princess?" Nick asked, obviously confused. "Oh, shit, baby. Are you sick again?"

Disgusted and still pissed off at him, she snapped, "Can't get anything past you, Einstein, can I? How about giving me some privacy, Nick, and then you can have the bathroom to hose all the booze off since you reek of it."

Nick seemed to be deep in thought over her suggestion. "Are you finished being sick?"

"Yes, I'm okay now. I just need a minute to make it back to bed." She swayed on her feet as she tried to stand up too fast. Nick was by her side in an instant. Despite her protests, he swung her up in his arms effortlessly and walked into the bedroom to deposit her on the bed. Without saying a word, he went to the kitchen and returned with a glass of water and a wet cloth. She sat quietly while he cleaned her face and held the glass to her lips.

For someone who had been slurring his words a few minutes ago, Nick seemed to have sobered up fast.

"You need to go to the doctor tomorrow, baby. This is two nights in a row that you have been sick."

"I'm fine, Nick. I'm sure it will pass." Wrinkling her nose at the smell of liquor on his breath, she said, "Why don't you go home and sleep it off?"

"I'm not leaving you here sick. But I will go shower since it offends you so much."

Before she could stop herself, she blurted out, "Where were you tonight?"

"What do you care, princess? Did you have an itch that you needed scratched? Because I know that's the only reason you ever want me around."

Beth saw red. Was he actually complaining about having sex with her now? She wanted to hit him with something. Instead of physically assaulting him though, she hit him where she knew it would hurt him the most. "No, you ass. I'd just rather the father of my baby not wrap his car around a tree because he is stupid enough to drive while drunk!"

Nick gave her a smug smile and said, "I took a cab so get off your high horse." He stood up and walked into the bathroom.

Beth sat in the bed, stunned. He had made no comment at all about the first part of her sentence. Was he so drunk that he hadn't understood what she said? She finally worked up the nerve to tell him and this was it? No shock? No nothing?

Suddenly the bathroom door flew open and Nick

stood there with no shirt on and just his pants riding low on his hips. She could hear the shower running. His face was white and his eyes were wild. "What did you just say?" he whispered.

"Um, that I didn't want you to drive while you were drunk?" Beth hedged.

"No, before that," Nick responded quietly.

"I didn't want the father of my baby to wrap his car around a tree." Beth closed her eyes when she saw the reaction on his face that she had expected when she first delivered her bombshell.

She heard Nick clear his throat and then, "I'll be right back."

He was back about ten minutes later having obviously showered. He had pulled on a pair of lounge pants that he kept at her place to wear in the evenings. He looked stone-cold sober as he settled in a chair near her bed.

Beth was starting to get unnerved as he continued to stare at her. Finally realizing that he was waiting for her to say something, she cleared her throat and tried to think of where to begin. "I'm pregnant and it's yours." *Smooth, Beth, real smooth. You couldn't start with a flowery speech? I think he already knows you're pregnant and that he's the father.* "I . . . I just found out. I was going to tell you tonight, but you didn't come home."

"How? I thought you were on the pill?"

"I am. God, I don't know. I could have missed one, I

just don't know." She looked down to buy time, picking an imaginary piece of lint off the bedspread while she waited for him to freak out and start accusing her of trying to trap him.

"This is why you've been sick the last few nights, isn't it?" Then, almost as if it were an afterthought, he added, "I thought it was called morning sickness?"

Beth managed a strained laugh, saying, "Yeah, I seem to have that backward. I hope this isn't going to happen every day because it's a horrible feeling to wake up in the middle of the night deathly sick."

With a grimace, Nick said, "I'm sorry I didn't make it for dinner. I just had a lot on my mind. I wasn't with anyone though, so don't even think that."

"I wasn't, but thanks for clarifying. I know we aren't exclusive so you don't owe me explanations, but I would like the courtesy of a call the next time."

"Beth, you are carrying my child; I'd say that's pretty damn exclusive." Without waiting for her response, he walked over to the other side of the bed and slid in. Turning off the light, he rolled over and gathered her loosely into his arms, kissing her gently on the forehead. "We'll figure it out, princess."

She snuggled against his warmth, too surprised to say anything else. Was he still in shock? He was taking this much better than she could have imagined. Maybe he was still too drunk to process everything. Tomorrow morning it would hit him, right?

*   *   *

Nick lay in bed awake long after Beth drifted off beside him. He curved his hand around her still-flat stomach as if looking for evidence of the life inside it. When she had dropped the bomb earlier, it really hadn't sunk in until he was about to step into the shower. He froze when he realized the enormity of her statement. *The father of my baby.* Damn, life had just taken a very sudden and unexpected turn. She had looked ready to bolt while she waited for his reaction. What had she expected him to say? He needed time to process everything.

He could imagine how Suzy and Gray were going to react to the news. Especially after their narrow escape with Reva a few months back. Things were different with Beth, though. He knew she wouldn't lie and deliberately try to trap him. Hell, she did everything she could to keep some distance between them.

There was no way Beth would try to get pregnant. He had tried to form a bond with her, and she was either afraid or just didn't want to be tied down to him. He had yet to figure out which. She sure wanted the sex. That was never in question. At times he thought he had caught her looking at him with what appeared to be affection. But he still couldn't really work out how she felt toward him. Plus, he didn't know what he felt; he just knew he wanted her in his life right now.

Was he ready to be a father? *Ready or not, it's going to happen. Oh, man, don't let it be a girl. I'll spend my whole life trying to keep men like me away from her.*

Beth tangled her legs with his, snuggling further against him as she always did while she slept. She might keep her distance during the daylight, but at night, her body sought him out in the dark and curled around him, night after night.

Chapter Six

"How soon do you want to get married?"

Beth spit her orange juice across the table, narrowly missing Nick's crisp white shirt. "Wh— What are you talking about?" she sputtered.

Without looking up from his morning newspaper, Nick said, "Well, since we're having a baby, we're getting married, princess. We also need to look at houses; this apartment is too small."

Beth was speechless for a moment before she blurted out, "We're not having a baby—*I'm* having a baby and I don't need to get married for that."

Nick looked at her in surprise and then spoke slowly to her, as if he were talking to a child. "Honey, this is *our* baby and I plan to be a very hands-on father. I don't intend for my baby to have a different last name nor do I plan for him, or her, to wonder where Daddy is every day. Any ideas on where you want to have the wedding?"

"I'm not buying a house or marrying you! Have you lost your mind? This isn't the Dark Ages where you have to marry the little woman because you knocked her up. Nick, I'm perfectly capable of handling this by myself. You can see the baby anytime you like."

She had Nick's full attention now as he slapped the newspaper on the table. "Why even bother telling me, Beth? It seems like you have everything all figured out." Standing up, Nick bent over until they were face-to-face. "Well, you know what, princess? I'm not going anywhere. You aren't pushing me away from my child. Maybe I'm not who you envisioned in this role, but I'm who you've got and you better learn to deal with it."

With one final glare at her, Nick stalked off. Beth heard the front door slam and she slumped back against her chair. *What just happened? He wants to get married? Could he still be drunk this morning?* Boy, was he pissed off. What had he expected her to say? Sure, every girl dreams of such a romantic proposal. *Hey, little woman, let's get hitched this weekend. I want you barefoot and pregnant and in my home by nightfall. Ohhh, stop, Nick, you smooth-talking sex god, I can't take any more! Okay, so the sex god part is accurate. But down, girl. Don't get distracted by the countless orgasms he has given you. Focus on the big picture. He is not forever-after material. There is nothing there but heartache.*

Nick was sadly mistaken if he thought he was pushing her into marrying him. With a glint in her eyes, she picked up her cell phone and checked her missed calls. She had twenty-nine. A few were from Suzy and Ella, but the rest were from men who actually *were* marriage material, at least their profiles said they were. She had signed up with a dating service before she met Nick and recently reactivated her profile—now seemed like a good time to put some distance between herself and Nick. She needed to show Nick that, although she was carrying his child, she was still an independent person who made her own decisions. He had better call a halt on purchasing a new house or a minivan because she wasn't marrying him. She was moving on with her life.

She ruthlessly shushed the voice in her head that asked, "What in the hell are you thinking? Pregnant women shouldn't be making dates for every night this week." She needed to focus on the future.

When Nick roared into the parking lot at Danvers a short time later, he spotted his brother leaning against his car waiting for him. He wanted to keep driving. He really didn't want to hear the lecture that Gray was no doubt about to unleash on him. He parked and jumped out of his car. Might as well get it over with. At least Gray wasn't as likely to kick him in the balls as Suzy.

"Hey, bro, what's up?"

Gray studied him as if debating whether to say something or not. Finally, he asked, "Anything you want to talk about?"

With a resigned sigh, Nick said, "Just go ahead and spit it out. I know that everyone probably already heard that Beth's pregnant."

"Yeah. Suzy told me in a pretty colorful way." Gray laughed.

Clapping Gray on the shoulder, Nick said, "Sorry about that, man. I bet that was rough. I'm sure she plans to rip me a new one before the day is over."

"She was pissed, but she realizes that you aren't completely to blame. I think having to deal with the mental image of you and Beth on our kitchen counter was much harder for her than finding out that her sister was pregnant."

"Shit, how much did Beth tell you guys? Women really do share everything, don't they?"

Gray laughed at Nick's obvious embarrassment. It wasn't often that his confident brother looked uncomfortable where a woman was concerned. "Oddly enough, she was just trying to defend you. She basically said that you tried to resist, but she was determined to override you." As if realizing what he had said, Gray added, "Maybe *override* wasn't a good word to use."

Nick chuckled at Gray's poor choice of words. Then, taking pity on him, he decided to change the subject. "I told Beth this morning that we were going to get married and find a house. That seemed to really piss her off."

Grinning, Gray said, "Well, if you said it just like that I can't imagine why she wasn't jumping for joy. I'm constantly wondering why people think you are the smooth talker in the family."

"What the hell is this, Pick on Nick Day? What

should I have said, man? It's not as if she was going to believe a big declaration of undying love. I care about her too much to lie to her. I don't think either one of us saw this coming, but now that it has we need to make some plans."

Gray studied him quietly for a few minutes before asking, "You do understand that you are going to be a father, right? I was expecting a different reaction from you this morning. Maybe more pacing, profanity, and less calm acceptance. You've realized that marriage means monogamy?"

"Yes, smart-ass, I do. Despite your high opinion of me, I can actually be faithful to one woman. I have never screwed around while I've been involved with someone and, believe me, the opportunity has presented itself more than once."

"Being faithful for a few months is a lot different from a lifetime." Gray held up a hand to silence his protests. "I'm just saying that you can be a father to this baby without getting married. I don't want to see you and Beth trapped in a marriage that makes you both miserable. I know that you care about her, but make sure you are doing this for the right reasons. I almost messed up my whole life with this very thing, so I know what I'm talking about. I dodged a bullet, but if Beth is pregnant, then I damn well know that you are the father without question because Beth isn't Reva."

Nick felt his anger dissipate. He knew this was hitting a nerve with Gray and that he had his best interests at heart. He was just tired of first Beth and then Gray automatically counting him out. Why did everyone assume he would cut and run as soon as he found out? Was it a crime to have a long dating history? He had a demanding job that he excelled at and no one ever had to worry about him letting any of his business responsibilities slide. He never had to be told anything twice. He took the ball and ran with it every day. Granted, a baby was a hell of a lot more important than a job, but why did they automatically assume that he couldn't handle it? One thing was for certain: He would show them that there was more to Nick Merimon than just a good roll in the sack. But the first person he needed to prove that to was Beth.

Chapter Seven

When Beth walked off the elevator, Ella was standing right there, as if waiting for her. The two had met when Beth had started working at Danvers, and the changes in Ella since their first meeting were nothing short of amazing. Ella had been raised by strict religious parents and had been sheltered her whole life. She had looked and dressed like someone at least twenty years older than she actually was.

Since Beth had spent most of her life hiding behind her overweight appearance, she could recognize a cry for help when she saw it. She knew that Ella desperately wanted to fit in and that she didn't have a clue as to how to do it. Beth might have problems with her own self-esteem, but she had no such qualms about helping Ella find her inner goddess. And, boy, had they ever!

The woman who stood in front of her now bore little resemblance to the awkward person of just months ago. Ella practically radiated happiness. She was still nervous and shy when someone out of her small circle of friends spoke to her, but she had come such a long way. Ella's former mousy brown hair was now a chestnut color and hung down her back in a long, shimmering curtain. Her blue eyes captured one's attention immediately and her adorable dimples made people try even harder to make her smile. She was small and petite, and Beth simply loved her to pieces.

The elevator chimed before they could move away and Declan Stone stepped out. She saw Ella's face light up as if she were a child sitting on Santa's lap for the first time. For some reason, Ella was nervous around every man of her acquaintance except Declan. Like herself, Beth thought that Ella needed to get out there more, but she didn't think Declan was the ticket.

The man was hotter than Myrtle Beach on the Fourth of July, but there was something almost dangerous about him. You never saw him standing around chatting with others, nor was he connected romantically with anyone. The man was a machine. Everything he said was direct and to the point. According to Nick, he was flawless in business negotiations and well respected around the world.

The only person who seemed to thaw the ice surrounding Declan was the woman standing beside her, and Beth was both impressed and terrified for her friend. Ella tended to stammer a lot when men spoke to her, but with Declan, everything was effortless for her. Beth caught a glimmer of a smile on Declan's surprisingly lush lips when his gaze rested on Ella.

"Good morning, Declan," Ella enthused.

"Morning, Ella. I . . . hope everything worked out okay with your grandmother's procedure."

My god, this is priceless. He likes her. The Iceman actually likes Ella. Oh, shit, no! He will eat her for lunch and spit her out. She needs a man with training wheels to get her feet wet, not a man who started life as a Corvette.

"She did great, Declan, thank you for asking."

Clearing his throat and obviously uncomfortable to be having this conversation in front of Beth, Declan turned his gaze and finally acknowledged her presence. She got the more formal, "Good morning, Beth."

"Good morning, Declan. Ella, I'm going to go check in with Suzy. How about lunch today?"

Ella smiled and agreed immediately. When Beth turned the corner, she saw Ella and Declan still standing in the same spot. Ella seemed to buzz around him like a brightly colored firefly and Declan seemed helpless to look away. *Why are you worrying so much about Ella and Declan? It seems like you have more than enough problems of your own to keep you busy for a while. Ella's a big girl and there is no way Declan would get seriously involved with her. She is way too innocent for him.*

When she walked into her sister's office, Suzy was ramming papers in her red leather bag and cursing under her breath. Sparing Beth a quick glance when she closed the door, Suzy said, "I have to be across town in twenty minutes and I can't find my damn phone."

Beth smiled as she walked to the credenza behind Suzy's desk and unplugged her sister's iPhone. "I think you plugged it in here to charge."

"Why can't they make a phone that doesn't have to be charged? What's wrong with a twelve-month Duracell?" Suzy grumbled. "I'll be gone until after lunch. I'm going to check out the new conference facility for next month. Can you check with the suppliers and see where we are on our orders?"

"Yep, I have it on my list for this morning. You'd better get going. Traffic will be terrible at this time."

As Suzy started for the door, she turned and asked, "Did you tell him?"

"Yes, Mother, I did so you can stop worrying. He wants to get married and buy a house immediately. I told him no."

Suzy shook her head, clearly trying to process this latest development. "He wants to get married? Are you sure we're talking about the same Nick here? Oh, hell, don't say anything else. I'm going to be late and I'm terrified you will start talking about sex and I'm not strong enough for that this morning. We'll talk when I get back." Suzy slammed out the door and then almost immediately flung it back open. In a low but menacing whisper she said, "You'd better not have sex in my office . . . ever!"

Beth chuckled as she walked to her own office. She hoped Suzy's warning didn't extend to *her* office because if it did, she had already violated that one. Maybe after-hours sex didn't count.

When Ella tapped on her door at lunchtime, Beth was just hanging up the phone after another exhausting call from Nick. At this point, she would rather him freak out and run than stay in the methodical mode he was currently in. He seemed to have an accidental-pregnancy handbook from the 1960s and he was running through it step by step. Marry the little woman immediately. Buy a house immediately. Plan the next ten years of Junior's life immediately. She felt weak and dizzy after the last call, and it had nothing to do with morning sickness and everything to do with Nick suffocating her. No matter how much she protested, he just kept going on as if he hadn't heard her. Was it really so hard for him to imagine a woman not dying to marry him? *Um, yeah, you probably are one of the few women alive who wouldn't jump at the chance.*

"Tough day?" Ella gave her a sympathetic smile as she perched on the corner of Beth's desk.

Dropping her head onto her desk, Beth said, "You have no idea. The man is making me crazy. I just want a moment to breathe, but he is after me constantly. I haven't even had a chance to come to terms with it myself and he is pushing me relentlessly."

Ella patted her back consolingly while making murmurs of agreement. "Grab your purse and let's walk around the corner for lunch. Getting out of here for a while will help."

Beth gave her friend a grateful smile as she gathered her stuff. "That sounds great, but I'm warning you now. If we see Nick anywhere on the way out, be prepared to run for your life because I am not talking about the advantages of breast-feeding anymore today, I mean it!" She heard Ella's groan of disbelief behind her as they walked to the elevator. "You only think I'm kidding. He's already tried to talk me into natural childbirth, too. Someone needs to stop the man from doing any more Google searches about pregnancy."

Chapter Eight

Nick opened Beth's apartment door that evening with the key that she had given him a few months back. Since their schedules were often different, it had made sense to be able to come and go as needed. She also had a key to the penthouse where he was staying.

He laid his briefcase down on the breakfast bar that separated the kitchen from the dining area. He noticed the blinking light on her answering machine that indicated a message. In all of the months that he had been in her apartment, he had never seen a message light blinking on the machine. He knew it was none of his business and an invasion of her privacy, but he couldn't seem to look away from the flashing light. Maybe it was something concerning the baby.

He managed to pull himself away from the machine without pushing the button to hear the message and walked to the bedroom to find Beth. She was curled up on top of the comforter on the bed sound asleep. She took his breath away. He didn't know how long he stood in the door just watching her. She looked so young and so vulnerable in sleep. The need he felt to protect her since he had learned she was pregnant was suddenly overwhelming. She looked so small lying there that it was hard to believe their child was nestled inside her.

In between meetings and conference calls, he had spent his day reading everything he could on pregnancy. Truthfully, a lot of it had scared the shit out of him. He had so much sweat on his face at one point that his secretary had asked him if he was feeling okay. He had wanted to yell, *"Hell, no, I'm not feeling okay. Beth is carrying a ticking bomb. A million things could happen to her or the baby. Oh, God, I'm having chest pains. Am I too young for a heart attack?"* Instead, he had offered her reassurance that he was far from feeling ill and then called Beth for the tenth time to see how she was feeling.

Now, standing here and looking at the beautiful woman resting so peacefully, he once again felt his chest go tight. He knew she couldn't hear him but he made the promise anyway. *"I won't let you down, Beth. I'll be the best husband and father that I can possibly be. Just give me a chance to prove it. You will never want for anything. I'll lay the world at your feet. Just believe in me, please."*

Nick quietly shut the door behind him and walked into the kitchen for a beer. The light on the answering machine was again calling to him. *You really should check it. What if there is a family emergency? She would want to know immediately. You would be doing her a favor.* Before he could talk himself out of it, he grabbed a pen and a notepad to write down the message and pushed the button.

"You have two new messages. First message today at four twenty p.m. Hey, Beth, it's Seth. I wanted to make sure that we're still on for dinner tomorrow night. Please give me a call and let me know. I'm looking forward to seeing you again." The next message was also from Seth leaving his cell phone number in case Beth had lost it.

Who in the hell was Seth and what was with the *"Looking forward to seeing you again"*? Had Beth been out with this guy recently? Nick felt something completely alien take control of him: jealousy. Maybe they hadn't formally talked about making their relationship exclusive, but he had assumed they were on the same page. He didn't date other women when he was involved with someone. Had Beth been dating? She was late coming home from time to time and she did mention going out to dinner with friends but at the time he thought she meant women friends.

Seth's intimate tone on the message didn't sound like that of a buddy. It sounded like a guy excited about seeing a woman. *Well, she didn't have any problem letting you know that she wanted you, did she? You may not be the only ticket in town, my friend.*

*   *   *

Beth rolled over in bed surprised to see how dark the room was. A look at the clock showed that she had been asleep for almost two hours. Despite the nap, she still felt fatigued. The morning sickness was taking a toll on her body. With another quick stretch, she slid her legs off the side of the bed and went to the bathroom to wash her face and straighten her hair.

Looking much more presentable, she walked into the living room and stopped short at seeing Nick sitting on one of the barstools deep in thought. She took a deep breath and allowed herself the pleasure of just looking at him. God, the man was beautiful. She had the urge to rip his clothes off every time he was anywhere near her and now was no exception. Her body tightened with need as she slowly approached him.

As if sensing her, Nick's head shot up. Beth stopped in her tracks at the look of confusion and sadness on his face. Something was obviously wrong. She reached out to take his hand and he moved his away. She dropped her hand back to her side and asked quietly, "What's wrong?"

Instead of answering her question, he held up a slip of paper and snarled, "Who is Seth?"

Beth drew a complete blank. "Um, Seth who?"

Nick tossed the piece of paper down in disgust and jumped to his feet. "Beth, don't you have anything a little more original than that?"

Had he lost his mind? Maybe he was drunk. Where was the happy-go-lucky Nick that she was used to?

This Nick was cold, angry, and, damn him, a complete turn-on. She wanted nothing more than for him to slam his mouth down onto hers and take her hard and fast. Talking slowly as she might to a child, she said, "I really have no idea what you're talking about. You aren't making any sense."

Never breaking eye contact with her, he pushed a button behind him and played the messages on her answering machine. When the second message finished, she couldn't hold it in any longer. A giggle escaped her and then another until she was doubled over laughing so hard that tears were streaming down her face. Instead of looking at her in anger now, Nick was just looking at her as if she were insane.

He didn't say a word as she mopped up the tears that had been running down her cheeks. "Sor— Sorry, give me a minute." Beth chuckled once more and took another breath to steady herself. Grinning at him standing there with his arms crossed and frowning at her, she asked, "So that message brought this whole he-man routine out?"

"I'm glad you think it's so funny, Beth, because I'm still not amused. Who is Seth?"

Shrugging her shoulders, she walked to the kitchen for a drink of water. "He's just a guy I went out with before, no big deal."

"How do you know him and when did you go out with him?"

Still unable to figure out why he would be upset, she

replied, "I, um, met him through a dating service and we went out a few weeks ago."

Nick turned to face her, his face thunderous. "You're using a dating service and you've been seeing this guy while we've been together?"

Suddenly it hit her how bad this whole thing must look to him. True, they hadn't made any promises, but they had, for all intents, been spending most nights together. *Well you wanted to put some distance between you, here's your chance. If you really want to lose him, you can do it right now.* Faking a carefree manner that she was far from feeling, she said, "I never said I wasn't seeing other people, Nick. I assumed you were as well. I signed up for the dating service months ago. Before you even ask though: Yes, I do know for sure that I am carrying your child."

"I wasn't going to ask that, Beth. I know you wouldn't lie to me about something like that. Tell Seth and anyone else you're seeing that it's over. You're pregnant and getting married. There seems to have been some confusion about seeing other people while we are dating, but let me clear it up for you. I'm not sharing my girlfriend, and I'm sure as hell not sharing my wife and the mother of my child. Send the memo, princess, you're off the market."

"You're crazy! I'm not marrying you and you can't tell me what to do. I'm an adult, Nick. You don't own me. In fact, I plan to go out with Seth tomorrow night."

Nick stared at her, clearly mystified over her refusal to make their relationship exclusive. Someone perfect like Nick could never understand the insecurities that someone like Beth harbored. He was too perfect for her. She would constantly find herself flawed against his perfection. She was pregnant and, God help her, about to start gaining some of her hard-lost pounds back. How would he feel when he could no longer span her waist with his hands? Would he enjoy her breasts as much when they were too large and far more than the current handful? Would he want to kiss and caress her lips as much when there was a double chin below them?

Nick prowled toward her and she took a step backward, suddenly nervous at his intense expression. When he had her backed up against the wall, she laughed nervously. "What're you doing?" He ignored her question and lowered his head to her neck. She felt his warm lips slide against her sensitive skin and she gave an involuntary shudder. "Nick—"

His tongue thrusting into her mouth silenced the feeble protest she attempted to make. With a groan, she surrendered to him. They both knew she was powerless to resist how he made her feel. At that moment, she would have followed him off a cliff, so she issued no denial when he backed her toward the bedroom, never once breaking contact with her mouth. *Just one more time and I'll be stronger the next time. Everyone deserves a weak moment, right?* Even as she repeated the reassurances to herself, Beth had to wonder if she would ever be strong enough to walk away from this man who took her breath away and set her body on fire with just one look. *Would it be so bad to take what he's offering?*

Chapter Nine

Beth had worked steadily through the morning, and she stood up behind her desk stretching her tired muscles. It was probably the workout from last night that had her fatigued the most. My God, that man knew how to use his tongue and the rest of him wasn't too shabby, either. She hadn't realized how lost in her thoughts she was until a snort from the doorway startled her back to the present.

Suzy, Ella, and Claire stood there looking at her. Suzy looked disgusted, Claire looked amused, and Ella looked as she always did, supportive. "Ugh, I know that look. She's either thinking about the last time she got lucky or she just got lucky in her office. Just for the record, Claire, as an owner of this company, now objects to any sexual activity in her building, right, Claire?"

Claire looked at Suzy and laughed. "Um. . . . Sure, yes, whatever she says."

Beth stuck out her tongue at Suzy and grabbed her purse to join them. They all chatted about their mornings until they were in Suzy's SUV. Suzy turned in her seat and looked over at her sister sitting in the rear seat. "Let's go ahead and address the elephant in the room. I told Claire you have a bun in the oven. You know I suck at keeping secrets from her. Now all of us know and you don't have to sit through lunch wondering."

She could feel her cheeks flushing as Claire gave her a sympathetic look. Ella, bless her heart, quickly changed the subject. The conversation was light and easy and Beth was just starting to relax after placing her lunch order when Suzy decided to move in for the kill. "So, what's the status on the whole marriage, white-picket-fence thing that Nick's trying to sell you?"

You really had to give Claire credit. She didn't even look surprised by her best friend's abrupt question. Ella was looking like she wanted to crawl under the table. She still hadn't gotten used to Suzy's direct way of getting straight to the point. "Nothing's really changed; he still wants to marry me, but I told him it's not gonna happen. Boy, if you think he was pissed off over that, you should have seen his expression when I told him I was still going on my date tonight with Seth. Now, that was a Kodak moment if I've ever seen one."

"Whoa, wait a second. Who's Seth?" Suzy demanded.

Beth immediately cringed. *Way to go, Big Mouth. Now you've moved Suzy up to DEFCON, level 5. Lie or tell the truth? Crap, he's probably already told Gray, so you might as well come clean.* "Um, just a guy from the dating service." *Have you lost your mind? No one else knows about the dating service!* Three sets of eyes were riveted on her and she fought the urge to slap her hand across her mouth in horror.

"Shit, I need a drink. Someone might have to drive us back to work because I don't think I can handle any more of this story sober," Suzy said, groaning. Beth thought she was kidding until she flagged a waiter down and ordered a *grande* margarita. She held her hand up to keep everyone silent until the large drink was sitting in front of her. After a dramatic gulp, she said, "All right, let's hear it."

Nervously stirring her drink with a straw, Beth said, "I . . . I, um, joined a dating service a while back. It's no big deal. I just wanted to meet some new people."

Looking stunned, Suzy asked, "You joined a dating service while you were sleeping with Nick?"

"Oh, no, it was right before. Since Nick and I aren't really in a relationship, I've still been dating casually." *Oh, God, they are all staring at me. Why did Ella look so shocked? She knew about the dating service. Beth had even tried to talk Ella into joining with her.*

"Sis, I'm not a cheerleader for Nick or anything, but how can you still be dating when you are involved with him? Doesn't he notice how often you are busy?"

"It's usually only once or twice a week. He just assumes I'm with Ella. I'm not lying to him; he just doesn't ask," she defended herself.

With a smile, Claire said, "Well, in his defense, he is

Nick Merimon. As much as I love my husband and as sexy as he is, I can still appreciate the fact that Nick is hot, hot! It probably never occurred to him to think that you were seeing anyone else. I'm betting this is the first time . . . ever. Just out of curiosity, why are you automatically counting him out? You obviously have feelings for him or you wouldn't be practically living together. Why won't you give him a chance? He's said he wants to marry you and raise this baby with you."

Beth's shoulders suddenly slumped as she whispered what she already knew. "Because he'll leave. I can't let myself get attached to him. I know I am not the type of woman that someone like Nick will end up with."

"Has he said something to you?" Suzy demanded. "I'll kick his ass. Who does he think he is running my sister down? You're way too good for him!"

Suzy was getting to her feet, her face enraged, but Beth managed to pull her back down. "No, no it's not that. Nick has never said anything negative to me." Looking down, she added, "He seems to love my body . . . a lot. I just know it won't last, though. I've always known that we were short-term."

"My God," Suzy said. "You've continued to date this whole time so you would have someone to rebound with immediately, in case Nick left. You never intended for him to last this long, did you?"

This lunch seemed to be going from bad to worse. Beth was never comfortable being the center of attention, even around her closest friends, and Suzy, Claire, and Ella hadn't stopped staring at her since she dropped the dating-service bomb. She knew that they weren't judgmental people, but she could see the shock and another emotion she knew well: pity. "Guys, it's not that bad. Nick and I have a good time and when he leaves, life will go on. He'll see the baby whenever he wants to. I would never deny him that right. I just can't get caught up in what he's selling. Soon, the new-baby glow will wear off and he will be looking for a way out. I refuse to be a stage-five clinger like all the other members of the Nick Merimon Fan Club."

Suzy chuckled beside her. "Stage-five clinger? God help you, Beth, because you are my sister through and through. Hell, you actually shock me on a regular basis now, and I didn't think that was possible. So you're testing Nick now to see if he'll run? Aren't you? Maybe a little torture? No boom-boom? Making him jealous?"

"Um, no, I'm not doing that." Then with a laugh of her own, she said, "There is no way I can withhold the boom-boom. I never get enough of him."

"Ugh, TMI! Please don't say anything else. I can't get drunk since I have to go back to the office, and this sure isn't a conversation I can deal with sober," Suzy moaned.

Beth took pity on Ella since she was already almost crimson with embarrassment. Ella had confided in her that she was still a virgin and Beth knew that she was easily embarrassed, especially over anything concerning sex. She patted her on the hand and whispered, "Sorry, Ella."

Ella gave her a shy smile in return and said, "Are you kidding? This is like watching a live taping of *Days of our Lives* or *Desperate Housewives*."

Everyone around the table laughed and kept it light while they finished eating. When they were waiting for their bill, Claire looked at Beth with what could only be called an evil smile. "So, Beth, I have an idea. You say that Nick will cut and run when things get tough. I've got the perfect way to give him a little test." Beth wasn't sure if she wanted to know, but she let Claire continue. "You know Mom and Tom are on their honeymoon, and Louise and her sister have gone to Florida for a few weeks. Jason and I would really love a date night, and we wouldn't trust just anyone with Chrissy."

Suzy looked at her friend in admiration. "Ohhhh, I like where you're going here. Hey! If you need a babysitter, why haven't you asked me? Gray and I are perfectly capable of babysitting."

Claire threw an arm around her friend's shoulders and laughed. "The last time I was at your house you set my diaper bag and purse on the sidewalk when Chrissy started crying."

"Hey, I couldn't see you pop your boob out one more time. The kid's going to choke on that thing, or something. Those babies are never going airborne again after the workout she's giving them."

Ella looked even more mortified if that was possible. Beth quickly asked Claire, "You would actually trust us to babysit for you? You know we don't actually have much baby experience."

"I trust you completely, Beth. You were an elementary schoolteacher for years. We can go over all of the details and I'll run you through her routine. She goes to bed early so you guys wouldn't be on duty the whole time. If you want to see how Nick is around a baby, this is a perfect chance."

"Hmmm, okay. Why not? I might as well start getting some practice in, and Nick needs to know what he is trying to get himself into. How about Saturday night?"

Claire smiled. "That sounds great. Jason will be so excited. It will be nice to go to a restaurant to eat without spit-up all over us. I don't think we've had a conversation since the baby was born that didn't involve the contents of her diaper. Maybe we should just use our date time to catch up on our sleep in the car."

Suzy snickered. "That's just sad. It must be depressing to have a stallion that you never have the energy to ride."

Ella almost fainted when Claire smiled and said, "Oh, honey, my stallion is never in the stable. I'm never too tired to give him a good workout."

Beth grabbed Ella's elbow and pulled her out of her chair. "Let's go before you're ruined forever."

She was surprised when Ella said, "Oh, man, I just

love them. I didn't know that Claire had a horse, though."

Beth's mouth dropped open in shock. Surely, Ella wasn't *that* naive. When Ella doubled over in laughter and said, "Got ya," Beth had to admit that her shy little friend had certainly come a long, long way.

Chapter Ten

Beth was relieved to see that Nick wasn't at her apartment when she arrived home. She didn't know who she thought she was fooling by insisting that they didn't live together because he was always here, and she didn't even question it anymore.

She quickly showered and pulled on a black jersey dress that landed just above her knees. It was sleeveless with a daring neckline. She pulled on some black sandals that added inches to her height. A pair of simple silver hoops and a matching necklace completed the look. She was supposed to meet Seth at one of her favorite seafood restaurants in half an hour. She grabbed her purse and gave a prayer of thanks that she had avoided a confrontation with Nick.

Seth was waiting for her in the lobby of Sara J's. Beth just loved the restaurant's beautiful view overlooking the marsh in Garden City, South Carolina. She summoned up her best "date smile" as Seth leaned in to kiss her lightly. "You look beautiful, Beth. I'm happy to see you again."

Seth Jackson was tall and thin. He had sandy blond hair that he kept neatly trimmed and groomed. He was the manager for one of the bigger hotels on the Grand Strand, and he was always trying to convince her to come take advantage of the many amenities that it offered. He placed a polite hand at the small of her back as he led her to the hostess stand. The restaurant was crowded, as usual, but they were quickly seated at a table on the outdoor patio.

"I thought you might enjoy dining outside this evening."

"This is lovely; I'm glad you thought of it." Conversation with Seth was always easy and uncomplicated, just as life with him would probably be. He was attentive, polite, and funny. He didn't set her on fire like Nick did, but he wasn't likely to burn her in the end, either. She ordered a glass of tea and Seth ordered a glass of red wine. When their drinks were delivered, she took a sip of hers and smiled at Seth as he regaled her with tales of the more unusual hotel guests in the last few weeks.

The hair on the back of her neck started to prickle as she felt someone watching her. She looked around, not noticing anything unusual. *You're paranoid. Who would be watching you?* When nothing out of the ordinary happened, she finally loosened up and enjoyed herself.

When the door to the outside area opened, her mouth fell open. Sauntering toward her, looking like the devil himself, was none other than Nick. She knew what she must look like to Seth. She had stopped talking in mid-sentence and was now gaping at the man approaching their table. *I wouldn't hold out much hope of another dinner invitation anytime soon.*

Nick smiled as he reached their table. He laid his hand on her shoulder in a proprietary manner. "Wh— What are you doing here?" she stuttered.

"Hey, princess. I was having dinner with a customer."

She looked around suspiciously, seeing no one waiting for him. As if he knew what she was thinking he added, "They've already left. I happened to see you when I was leaving, so I thought I'd come say hello." Leaning over her shoulder, Nick extended his hand toward Seth. "Nick Merimon."

She could see that Seth was very curious about their exchange as he politely shook Nick's hand and introduced himself. "So, how do you two know each other?" he inquired.

"We work together," Beth answered quickly.

"We also live together and Beth is having my baby," Nick added helpfully.

Beth watched in horrified fascination as Seth's uncertain smile slowly slipped off his face as he noticed the embarrassment on hers. "Beth? Is this true?"

With a weak smile, she said, "We don't officially live together; it's complicated."

"That wasn't really the part I was asking about," he said.

She knew her face was flaming as she searched for an answer that wouldn't sound as damning as the truth. "Er, yes, I am pregnant," she admitted, "But we aren't in a relationship or anything so I can see other people." *Oh, my God, just shut up. Do you hear yourself? You have just given new meaning to the expression "white trash."*

Seth stood up from the table, now completely flabbergasted. "I think you two need some time alone. Beth . . . good luck." With those words, he left as if the hounds of hell were nipping at his heels.

Nick walked around to take the recently vacated chair as she hissed, "What in the hell was that?"

"I don't know what you mean, princess. If you wanted me to lie for you, then you should have warned me ahead of time. I was just answering his question honestly."

Getting to her feet, Beth snapped, "Well, bravo for you then. I'll leave you here to revel in your honesty." She saw Nick hastily throw some bills on the table as he followed her out. When he reached over to pluck her keys out of her hand, she rounded on him, full of fury. "Give me my keys, Nick; I just want to go home."

All signs of humor were gone from his handsome

face as he said, "You're too upset to drive. I'll take you home and we can pick up your car in the morning."

"I'm fine! Just give me back my keys."

She sucked in a breath as he laid his hand against her stomach. "That's our child in there, Beth. I'm not letting you tear out of here while you're this upset. I'd never forgive myself if you had an accident and you or the baby was hurt."

All of the fight left her as her anger deflated. How could he drive her so crazy one moment and then say something like that in the next moment? He put a hand on the small of her back and gently led her toward his car. When he had her settled in the passenger seat, he walked around to the driver's side and slid in.

They drove across town in silence. She was relieved to escape to her bedroom when they reached the apartment. She desperately needed a few moments to herself to come to grips with the train wreck that was her life. She couldn't believe that Nick had rolled out their dirty laundry for the world to see tonight. Seth wasn't likely to ever speak to her again. The look on his face had been priceless. Just thinking about it made her start to laugh. Then, once the laughter started, she couldn't seem to stop. Nick stuck his head in the doorway, looking at her as if she had lost her mind. It only made her laugh harder. Soon tears were coursing down her cheeks as she fought to take a breath.

"Um, princess, are you okay?"

Suddenly her laughter turned into tears. His concern

was her undoing. The enormity of her situation was finally hitting home. Nick sat down on the bed and gathered her into his arms. He cradled her like a child, stroking her hair and murmuring soft words of comfort as she continued to sob. "I'm sorry, baby; I shouldn't have done that to you. I . . . I didn't know you liked that guy this much."

"It's not that," she mumbled. "That was actually kinda funny. I'm scared, Nick. I'm having a baby and Suzy's right; this is a life-changing moment. Everything's changing and I don't know if I'm strong enough to handle it." She took a hesitant look at his face, afraid of what she would see there. *He probably thinks I'm a pathetic basket case. All I do now is cry and throw up. If I were him, I would have my suitcase packed and waiting at the door.*

He grabbed a tissue from the nightstand and dried her tears. He kissed her on the forehead and pulled her back into his embrace. "I keep trying to tell you that I'm here for you. This isn't your baby, this is our baby. Why are you more than willing to go out with a man that you met through a dating service and give him a chance, but not me? We've been sleeping together for the last six months, but you'd rather trust a stranger than me?"

Oh shit, that really sounds bad. If I didn't know better, I would swear he's hurt. Has he ever given me reason to believe that I couldn't trust him? No. With a sigh, she pulled back to study him. "I'm sorry; you're right. I haven't handled this very well. You have to admit, you do have a bit of a reputation." *Really? You couldn't just apologize and make nice?*

Chuckling, he said, "I'm glad to see you're feeling better. As for my reputation, princess, I'm a man. I don't sleep with a different woman every night, but, yes, I have dated my share. Contrary to popular belief though, I'm not some kind of gigolo. I'm perfectly capable of being faithful to one woman. If you haven't noticed, you've had my full attention since the moment we met and I can't imagine that changing anytime soon."

He looked so sincere that she wanted to believe him. Maybe it was time to see what he really was made of. She would give him the chance that he seemed to want so much, but she wasn't going to make it easy. From now on, Nick would be involved up to his elbows. She would drag him to every doctor's appointment. They would be on a first-name basis with the employees of Babies-R-Us, where they would shop weekly until they found the perfect breast pump. She would ask him to rub her feet every night and cater to any cravings that she might have. First up though, they would babysit for Claire and Jason tomorrow night. If he made it through that, the games would begin. If he was still standing at the end, then she would beg him to marry her and never look back. *Be prepared—he's never going to make it. Don't let him break your heart. The man has left a trail of panties and broken hearts from here to Charleston. Don't forget it!*

She turned to straddle him and pressed a kiss to his mouth. "Okay, let's take it day by day. I can't promise anything, but I'm willing to try." Her heart stuttered as he turned a sexy smile on her. He looked so happy that she almost felt bad about what she planned to put him through. *No guts, no glory.* When his hand slid slowly up her leg to the curve of her bottom, her thoughts scattered.

Beth felt the hard line of his erection pressing into her stomach as she lost herself in his kiss. Unlike their usual frantic coupling, Nick set a gentle pace. He drove her wild as he lazily caressed her. By the time he moved over her and took possession of her body, she was almost out of her mind with need.

He drove into her gently, as if afraid she would break. His mouth covered hers, his tongue tentatively thrusting inside to stake claim. His kiss became wild and uncontrolled, completely at odds with his possession of her body. She wrapped her legs around his hips, forcing him deeper inside her. She was frantic for a release from the building pressure. Each time her body clenched and she was close to going over the edge, he pulled back, refusing to let her go over the other side. After his third retreat, she was so desperate that she sank her teeth into his shoulder. Suddenly, the maddening rhythm was gone and he lost all control. She hung on for dear life as his hips drilled into her and they both found the release that he had been denying them.

When she floated back to earth, she was certain about one thing; no matter what other problems they might run into down the road, sex would never be one of them.

Chapter Eleven

They arrived at Jason and Claire's a few moments before six the next evening. Nick looked completely at ease as they walked through the door. She had to envy his endless supply of confidence and easygoing demeanor. He seemed perfectly content to be spending his Saturday night babysitting.

Claire showed her Christina's room and how to make her bottles. Nick stood in the living room talking to Jason as if he hadn't a care in the world. When Claire and Jason had both kissed Christina good-bye, Claire gave Beth an evil smile and plopped the baby into Nick's arms. Jason smirked while Claire tried to cover her laugh with a cough. Finally, there was a crack in Nick's confident façade. He looked at Claire and asked, "So, are you guys sure about this? You know that we don't actually know anything about babies, right?"

Jason clapped him on the shoulder and said, "You'll be fine. We still don't know what the hell we're doing most of the time, but you learn. See you guys around midnight."

With another smirk, Claire followed Jason out the door.

As soon as the door closed, Nick held Chrissy out to Beth. She sidestepped him and walked to the couch to relax. Nick continued to stand in the entryway, obviously clueless about his next move.

"Come on over here and sit down." She smothered a laugh as he held the baby in front of him like a ticking bomb. When he gingerly settled onto the couch beside her, she gave him a round of applause. Chrissy picked that moment to smile at him adoringly and he was a goner. She saw him melt before her eyes as another female lost her heart to him.

"Hey, beautiful, are you from around here?" Chrissy grinned at him as if she knew exactly what he was saying. "So, do you want to go out and get a bottle or something one night?" Chrissy gurgled in delight. Apparently, you were never too young to appreciate a hot guy.

Nick looked at Beth and asked, "So, what do we do now, just sit here?"

"Pretty much. Claire said that she had already fed and bathed her. We'll put her down for bed in about an hour."

Nick grinned. "An hour? Man, we got off good. If we had held them off until seven we would be home free." He had barely finished his last sentence when all hell broke loose. One moment Chrissy was smiling and the next moment she looked like Linda Blair in *The Exorcist*.

My God, they call this a spit-up? It looks more like a nuclear explosion. Nick had vomit dripping down his shirt, running off his arms, and pooling in his lap. Chrissy was apparently thrilled to be rid of the load and cooed happily.

"Holy fuckamoly!"

"Nick! Watch your language."

"Princess, she can't talk. I have puke all over me; don't you think I deserve the satisfaction of some profanity?"

Beth started laughing but was silenced when he thrust the baby in her arms. "I've got to get this stuff off me before I add some of my own to it." Giving her an evil grin, he said, "Good luck, honey."

Wrinkling her nose at the foul smell, she carried Chrissy to her room and settled her on the changing table. She swiveled her little head around as if looking for Nick. "He'll be back soon, sweetie, and Auntie Beth will make sure he holds you again." She managed to strip the baby's clothes off and give her a quick bath with the warm baby wipes. Getting her dressed again was more challenging with her little legs kicking frantically. After ten minutes of getting one leg in just to have another kick out, Beth was about to give up. She was at her wit's end when Nick walked in with damp hair, wearing a T-shirt and shorts.

"I had to raid Jason's closet." Looking at the stains on Beth's shirt, he added, "You might want to look through Claire's."

"I will if I ever get Chrissy's clothes on. It's like trying to dress a wild animal."

Nick walked over and tickled Chrissy on the stomach, sending her off into a fit of giggles. "Here, you hold her up and I'll slip her legs in." Finally, with a little teamwork they had her dressed. Beth was exhausted and ready to collapse.

"Princess, go ahead and take a shower, you kinda smell. I'll rock the baby for a while."

Hesitating, she asked, "Are you sure you're okay alone with her?" *He is better at this than I am. I should make a break for it before he changes his mind.*

"We'll be fine. Don't take too long, though." Needing no further encouragement, she rummaged through Claire's drawers until she found a pair of jogging shorts and a matching top. She made quick work of the shower even though she was tempted to hide out in the bathroom for a while longer.

When she walked back into the baby's room, Nick was lying on the floor and Chrissy was sprawled on his chest. *Oh, dear God, he is doing baby talk to her.* She stood in the doorway watching her big and oh-so-sexy man say, "She's a good wittle girl, yesss, she is" and "Wonder what Wikipedia has to say about the word *wittle*?"

Nick finally noticed Beth standing at the door and,

instead of being embarrassed, he beckoned her to join them. Beth sat on the floor and laughed as he flew Chrissy like an airplane.

"Are you sure you've never been around a baby? Because you're a natural."

"Nope, but it's not so hard, right?" They both sniffed at the same time. "Hey, babe, do you smell something?" He was giving her a suspicious look.

"Hey! Don't look at me," she said indignantly.

"Well, it's not me." They turned their eyes to Chrissy in horror. "Oh, please, no," Nick whispered. "Check her, princess."

"Why me?" she snapped.

"I don't know, you're a woman, you know how to handle this crap. No pun intended."

"Just take her to the changing table and let's see what we're dealing with. It probably smells much worse than it actually is."

"Well, I hope so because it smells like death," he said, gagging.

Beth grabbed his arm as he tried to drop and run. "Oh, no, big guy, we're in this together. Grab a diaper and be ready."

"Should we put on gloves or something?" he asked.

"I . . . I don't know, do you see any?" Nick rummaged around, but came up empty-handed. "Just forget it, and let's get this over with before I'm sick." She quickly slid Chrissy's pants off and almost passed out at the sight that greeted her. The diaper looked huge and there was a distinct green outline around the leg openings.

"Damn! Is that normal? Nick gagged again. "What are they feeding the kid?"

"Just shut up and hand me some wipes. I'll open the diaper and you pull it out from under her on the count of three."

"Are you out of your mind? I am not pulling that thing. I'll open it and you pull the sucker."

She moved out of the way muttering, "Big baby."

Nick leaned away as far as he could before reaching for the tape on each side of the diaper. "Are you ready?" he asked.

"I guess. Just do it."

He pulled the tape and opened the diaper. She felt her stomach drop to her feet. "Oh, dear God. I can't Nick, I'll be sick if I touch that thing."

"Princess, if I have to pull the diaper out, then you're on butt duty."

"O-okay, I'll just put a lot of wipes over it. Go ahead and pull." As Nick removed the diaper and held it out like a bomb, she grabbed a wad of wipes and covered Chrissy's bottom.

"Beth, what do I do with this?" Nick asked frantically.

"Hey, I've got my own problems here." Nick circled the room looking more and more desperate for somewhere to dispose of the diaper. All of the bedrooms on the bottom level walked out onto the patio. When he walked over and wrenched the door open, she could only gape at him when he tossed the diaper over the railing. "Nick! You can't do that!"

"What? You told me to figure it out, well I did."

"But . . . you can't throw poop on the beach. You probably just broke at least ten laws. You've got to go get it." She turned her focus back to Chrissy's rump and was glad to see that it was almost clean. The stack of used wipes beside her was starting to resemble a landfill. Nick had washed his hands so she had him come over and hold the baby on the table while she washed up.

It again took a team effort to get Chrissy dressed. Beth picked the baby up off the table and said, "You've got to go get the diaper. Take a trash bag and put it inside."

"I'll hold the baby and you go pick it up," Nick pleaded. Then wiggling his eyebrows he added, "If you will, I'll give you the best sex of your life later."

Laughing, she said, "Oh, baby, you are so barking up the wrong tree right now. You've got nothing to offer me that would make me go pick that up. Be a man and suck it up. How are you going to change our baby's diaper if you can't even pick one up?" *Ah, yes, insulting the manhood always gets results. Try not to smirk.*

Beth was sure she heard some creative profanity as Nick headed off the deck with a large trash bag in his hand. She knew he had located the diaper when she heard him gagging, which continued all the way into the house. Nuzzling Chrissy's neck she said, "Now that's how you bring a big, strong man to his knees."

Nick came back with the bag and dumped it in the kitchen trash. He insisted on taking another shower and changing clothes. After a quick sniff of herself, she handed the baby off to him when he returned and showered again as well. When she came out in another one of Claire's outfits, both Chrissy and Nick looked sleepy. She fixed a bottle and Nick snuggled the baby against his chest, rocking her gently while she ate. *Oh, God, other than the diaper-throwing incident, he is better at this than I am. He doesn't seem scared at all.*

They walked into Chrissy's room together and tucked her into her crib. Beth left the door cracked so they could hear her if she woke up.

"I'm beat," she said as she flopped on the couch beside Nick. "How can it be only seven thirty? I feel like we have been here for days. How in the world are we ever going to take care of a baby twenty-four-seven?"

Nick patted her absently. "We'll get used to it. The first time is the hardest. Plus when it's your own kid, you know you don't have a choice."

"Yeah, I guess," she said doubtfully. She felt herself starting to nod off and dimly registered Nick slumping beside her.

*   *   *

Claire stood in front of the couch surveying the scene before her. Jason dropped his arm around her shoulders and she felt him shaking with laughter. "Man, look at that train wreck." Jason chuckled.

"Jason, stop. They helped us out so we could have a night out. They do look pretty rough though, don't they?"

"Rough is an understatement. Now I know how bad we must have looked for the first couple of months. No wonder everyone at work kept giving me that pitying expression. I must have looked like hell. Hey, are those my clothes?"

"Yep, and I think Beth has mine on. It looks like Chrissy showed them no mercy." Claire grabbed her cell phone from her purse and snapped a picture of the sleeping couple.

Jason asked, "What are you doing?"

Looking guilty, she said, "Um, I'm taking a picture to show Suzy. She's gonna love this. It looks like two homeless people crash-landed on our couch."

Jason kissed the tip of her nose and said, "Let's wake them up and get them out of here."

"Ah, maybe we should just let them sleep here; they look beat."

"It's your call, but I believe you promised to show me some of your old stripper moves tonight."

Claire's eyes widened and her breathing became heavy at seeing the desire in Jason's eyes. Suddenly she grabbed Beth's shoulder and started shaking her. "Time to go home, you two."

Jason quirked a brow at her. "I thought you wanted to let them rest."

"Screw that. Hurry up and help me wake them. I'll give you a bonus if you can get them out the door in less than five minutes."

Smiling in anticipation, Jason said, "You're on."

Chapter Twelve

Beth and Nick fell face-first onto the bed when they got back to the apartment. Neither of them mentioned making love. My God, she was barely pregnant and already their sex life was starting to suffer.

Claire and Jason had smirked at them when they had shaken them awake. When Beth pulled herself from bed to brush her teeth she got a glimpse of the reason. She did not even recognize the woman in the mirror. Her hair was standing up in every possible direction, her clothes were wrinkled and her mascara had smeared, making her look like a raccoon. *Ugh, just wash your face, brush your teeth, and try to tackle this in the morning. Nick probably looks like a million bucks.*

Nick was still lying in the same place when she crawled back into bed. She nudged him with her elbow, trying to roll him onto his side of the bed. "Hey, babe, move over. I'm hanging off the end over here." Suddenly, he sprang from the bed looking around the room wildly.

"Where's the baby? Oh, shit, we lost her!"

"What are you talking about? We don't have a baby yet." Suddenly, it hit her that he was still asleep. His eyes were open, but unfocused, and he was obviously upset. Lowering her voice to keep from startling him, she said gently, "Honey, we're home now. Claire and Jason have Chrissy and she's asleep in her crib. We didn't lose her." He still stood there clasping and unclasping his fists. *Great, what do I do now? Pour water over him? He'll probably punch me if I try to touch him. Let him stand there all night?*

Finally, she decided a loud noise might jolt him out of his sleep. Hopefully, it wouldn't give him a heart attack. She grabbed a book off her bedside table and heaved it at the closet door. The resulting crash sounded like the walls were caving in. *Maybe a little too much force behind the throw.* Nick jerked and looked around the room in confusion. She was relieved to see that he was really looking at her now and not through her. "What's wrong, baby?" he asked.

"You were dreaming and I was trying to wake you up. Do you normally talk and walk in your sleep?"

Nick looked at her in disbelief. "Um, no, I'm pretty sure I don't. Are you sure you weren't asleep yourself?"

"Nope, I was just coming back from the bathroom when you jumped off the bed and started trying to find the baby. I assumed you meant Chrissy." He still looked skeptical, but she was too tired to try to convince him. "I'm going to bed, why don't you get cleaned up, too."

*   *   *

Nick felt like his head had barely touched the pillow when Beth started moaning beside him. When he reached out to touch her, she jumped from the bed and ran into the bathroom. He winced in sympathy as he heard the now-familiar sound of her being sick. He hurried into the bathroom and lowered himself beside her. He pulled her hair back from her face and rubbed her back.

When she finally seemed to have nothing left, he picked her up and lowered her onto the sink counter where he washed her face and helped her rinse her mouth and brush her teeth. Seeing her like this made him want to cut his dick off. He really hoped that she was not sick like this the whole pregnancy because he didn't think either of them could survive. *She's the one having to puke her guts out every day; you're getting off easy.* She always allowed him to care for her after she was sick. She never complained as he cleaned her up and carried her to bed. He wrapped his arms around her and settled her against his chest. He kissed her neck and whispered, "I'm so sorry, princess. I'd take your place if I could."

Tonight had been something out of a horror story at times, but he had loved it. Taking care of Chrissy with Beth had shown him a glimpse of something he never thought he would want: a family. He knew it would be hard, but he also knew that eventually they would hit their stride and, after a while, the small stuff like being peed, pooped, and puked on wouldn't throw them as

much. Tonight they had resembled two circus mon-
keys, but it would not always be that way.

Now he just needed to keep his cool and show Beth
that he could handle anything she threw his way. Calm,
cool, and rational. He definitely had this.

Chapter Thirteen

"Whoa, where the hell are you putting that?" Nick demanded. They were at her first doctor's appointment and Nick spoke up just as the ultrasound technician raised the condom-covered probe toward Beth. *You're blowing it, buddy. What happened to calm, cool and rational? Get it together; they're staring at you.* Nick plastered on his default grin that never failed to charm. "Shouldn't you at least buy her a drink before you bring that thing out?"

Mindy, the ultrasound technician, chuckled and said, "You might as well get used to it, Dad. You'll have at least one more of the internal ultrasounds before we are able to switch to the external ones. The baby can only be viewed internally for the first few months. Remember, this is more uncomfortable for Mom than for Dad."

He really wished she would stop with the Mom and Dad stuff because it made them sound like her parents. He could tell by the smirk on Beth's face that she knew exactly what he was thinking.

Beth took a deep breath as Mindy inserted the probe. He quickly averted his gaze. "Okay, Mom and Dad, if you look at the screen you'll now see an image of the uterus. I'm just going to get some measurements and then we will continue on." After declaring Beth's uterus to be perfect, she continued. "Now, here is the yolk sac and the fetal pole. I'm just going to measure those as well so we can get an estimate of the baby's approximate age."

Confused, Nick asked, "What are a yolk sac and a fetal pole? Where is the baby?"

"The baby gets nourishment from the yolk sac at this point. The fetal pole is another word for the baby right now. They go through several different stages in the pregnancy. If we are lucky today, we will see the heartbeat as well."

Nick watched the screen in fascination as Mindy made her measurements. Beth looked shell-shocked. He took her hand, trying to give her the reassurance that she looked in desperate need of.

"Okay, Mom and Dad, let's see if we can find the heartbeat. You should see a little fluttering on the screen."

Suddenly, Nick saw a flickering on the screen and the room filled with a thumping sound. He looked at Beth and she had tears running down her face as they looked at their baby's heart beating. "Oh, yeah, there it is," Mindy said. "I thought so, but I wasn't sure until now."

"There what is?" Beth demanded. "Is something wrong with the baby?"

"Oh, no, Mom, the babies both look just fine."

"The babies?" Beth choked out. "You mean baby, right?"

"No, there are two babies in there. I thought I saw two yolk sacs, and there are definitely two heartbeats, see there?" She pointed to the two areas flicking on the screen. "Congratulations, you're having twins. How exciting!"

Nick didn't think it was possible for someone to look as green as Beth did at that moment. He should know because he felt the same way she looked. Twins? Heaven help them.

Oh my God! What have we done? How can we possibly handle twins? One baby kicked our ass last night. This can't be happening. I'll be huge. Oh, crap, I cannot believe I'm worrying about gaining weight. Focus on the big picture; you are having twins, with Nick!

"Princess, are you okay?" Nick's voice pulled her out of the fog that had descended over her after the declaration of twins. She looked around, realizing that Nick and Mindy were staring at her, waiting for a reaction. *I wonder what they would think if I passed out right here?*

"I . . . I'm fine. Just a little surprised." Looking at Nick, she continued, "Wow, twins, right?" *Why does he look so unruffled and cool? I am practically a stuttering mess and he looks like Mr. Hot Father-to-be. Mindy can't take her eyes off him. Back off, cougar, he's with me.*

Suddenly all business, Mindy handed them their first picture of the baby—or babies—and helped Beth up from the table. Beth went behind the curtain to get dressed and then met Nick in the hallway. "You can go back to the waiting room now and the nurse will call you back for your first appointment," Mindy said.

Before she thought about it, Beth blurted out, "Oh, God, there's more?" Mindy gave her a motherly pat on the shoulder and opened the door for them to the waiting room. She wasn't sure but she could have sworn that Mindy then gave Nick a not-so-motherly look of female appreciation.

They settled back into their seats in the waiting room. It seemed to Beth like every eye in the room was focused on Nick. Of course, it did not take much to figure out why. Most of the men who accompanied their wives or girlfriends were just Average Joes. Nick, on the other hand, looked like he could pose for *Playgirl* magazine. She hated to admit it, but she was proud to be sitting beside him. *Amazing. I am not jealous of these skinny girls anymore. I have a man beside me that they would all love to have. Score one for all of the former fatties in the world!*

Nick wrapped his hand around hers and brought it to his lips. "You know that everything will be okay, right? I know this is a lot to take in, but we can handle it. We need to look for a bigger place soon and we can hire some help if we need to. Claire and Jason will be happy to let us use Chrissy for more training. How about some of those baby classes, too?"

Beth finally put her hand over his mouth and said, "Please stop talking. I appreciate the reassurances, but I really want to make it home before I freak and if you keep talking that isn't going to happen."

"But—"

"No! Either you get me a bag to breathe in or we start talking about the weather. I cannot process things as fast as you can. Right now, all I can picture is my stomach dragging on the floor and my ass stuck in the door. You can solve all of our problems tomorrow; for right now just let me finish my panic attack."

Nick chuckled. "Okay, princess. I'll just read this breast-feeding magazine and keep my mouth shut."

Beth thought he was kidding until she caught sight of some pictures. They could put *National Geographic* to shame. She jerked the magazine out of his hands and muttered, "Just stare at the walls, please."

All too soon, the nurse was calling them back. Beth was mortified when the nurse stopped at a busy area and thrust a plastic cup in her hand. "Take this in the restroom there and give me a urine specimen. When you're finished bring the cup out with you." Then, handing her two packets, she continued, "Please wipe from front to back twice before gathering your specimen."

Oh, dear Lord. Weren't there supposed to be medical

privacy regulations? Now at least five people standing near her knew that she was going to pee in a cup and how she would be wiping before she did it. Nick leaned against the wall looking at her with amusement. She quickly entered the bathroom and shut the door. *How can I possibly pee knowing they are waiting for me? I'm a timid tinkler at the best of times.* She finally turned on the water full blast, hoping it would inspire her to go, as well as block out the noise in the hallway. After what seemed like an hour, she managed to collect a small amount in the cup.

The nurse looked at the cup disapprovingly, saying, "I hope this is enough."

Next, she was told to sit in a chair while the nurse drew three tubes of blood and stuck her finger. Finally, the nurse took a blood pressure cuff and wrapped it around her arm. Beth had so many bad memories about those things. When she was at her heaviest, the regular cuffs didn't fit. The nurses either tried to hold them on her arm, which ended with them popping open, or made Beth wait while they searched for a large cuff. The indignity of having that happen never got any less humiliating. Beth often wondered why all doctors didn't just use the larger cuff and save some of their patients from a lot of embarrassment.

Nick reached out to pat her shoulder, obviously picking up on her mood even if he didn't know the cause. She breathed a sigh of relief as the nurse finally let her up from the chair only to lead her directly to her

ultimate nightmare: the scales. Why had she not realized that this would happen? She would have made
Nick wait in the other room had she thought about
having to weigh in in front of him. She knew the number on the scales was acceptable and in normal range,
but it didn't lessen the nausea she felt every time she
stepped on.

She looked wildly around the area, hoping there was
a position that would give her some privacy. When she
saw the large, digital display on the wall above the
scales, she knew it was hopeless. *I can't get on the scales
in front of him, I just can't!* The nurse was waving her
forward impatiently as she looked at Nick. He raised
an eyebrow as if to ask what was going on. She didn't
want to voice her insecurities in front of the nurse, but
if she delayed any longer, the nurse was going to forc-
ibly pull her on the scales.

She felt Nick's hand at her back. "Honey, do you
mind if I walk down the hall to the water fountain
while you're finishing up here?"

Beth sagged in relief. She turned a grateful look on
him and said, "No, that would be great, thanks." He
gave her a smile of encouragement and walked quickly
down the hall and out of sight. She jumped on the scale
quickly and, as she always did in a doctor's office,
turned her head to keep from looking at the number.

Nick quickly walked away from Beth and didn't stop
until he rounded the corner, out of sight. His heart

squeezed at the look of pure terror on her face as she tried to avoid getting on the scales in front of him. It had taken him a minute to figure out why she was hesitating, even though the nurse was trying to rush her to step on. When she finally looked at him, he could see the panic in her eyes and it finally hit him. She seemed so confident to him, especially sexually, that it was hard for him to imagine her suffering from confidence or body-image issues, but she clearly did.

Suzy had warned him when he first moved in with them at Gray's that he'd better never say anything to Beth about her weight. Apparently, at one time, Beth had been overweight and Suzy was fiercely protective of her sister's feelings. It was a threat that was unnecessary. He had never been one to make fun of other people, even when he was in school, and he certainly would never do anything to upset Beth. She was a beautiful person, both inside and out, and, regardless of her size, she would still be a beautiful person to him. He had dated a variety of women in his time and, contrary to popular belief, not all of them were stick-thin models. He loved women with curves. He hated to take a woman to a restaurant and have them order water and a salad. It made him too self-conscious to enjoy his own meal.

Beth might never finish her meal, but at least she enjoyed all things in moderation. He knew she worked out regularly, which he admired. She had a stunning body and he practically drooled every time she walked by.

How would she be able to mentally handle the changes in her body that this pregnancy would bring? That was something that he hadn't even considered, but for Beth would it be more traumatic than the baby? He had never given a thought to how scared she might be to gain weight. Was there a way to recommend that she see a counselor without her blowing up at him? The terror in her eyes just a few minutes ago went far beyond the normal aversion that women had to telling their real age or weight. Maybe Suzy could give him some advice. *Yeah . . . maybe. Unless she still wants to cut off your penis for getting her baby sister pregnant.*

Chapter Fourteen

Nick and Beth drove straight to work from her doctor's appointment. The drive gave her some time to adjust to the shock of learning she was pregnant with twins.

Nick had been the loving partner that women dream of. When they met with her doctor, who was a very nice middle-aged woman who instantly made Beth feel comfortable, he had asked most of the questions. Since Beth was pregnant with twins, she would need to be more closely monitored as her pregnancy advanced. Nick had been intensely interested in everything the doctor had said. At one point, Beth found her head going back and forth just trying to follow the conversation between them. She had started to remind them that she was in the room, too. Dr. Winters clearly was charmed by Nick and thought Beth a lucky girl.

Ella was standing in the lobby of Danvers when she and Nick came in the front entrance. Beth gave him a quick kiss good-bye and walked over to join her friend. "Hey, Ella, are you just getting in, too?" Ella continued to stare across the room and Beth followed her gaze, curious as to what was holding her friend's attention. Across the lobby stood Declan with a striking blond woman who looked about Beth's own age and a very handsome man, wearing what Beth was sure was an expensive suit. Turning back to Ella she asked, "Who are those people with Declan?"

"I don't know," Ella whispered. "She's really pretty and she has her arm through Declan's. Do you think she's his girlfriend?"

Beth heard the note of despair in Ella's voice and wondered again what her relationship with Declan was. She had walked in on them talking frequently. Actually, Ella seemed to be the only one with whom Declan made small talk. "I don't know. I've never seen either of them around here before, but this is a big place so it could be a customer." As they continued to stand and stare, Claire walked through the door with Starbucks cups in hand. When she spotted them, she walked over with a smile on her face.

"Hey, you two. I was just bringing Jason some coffee. I'll admit he's getting pretty spoiled from me dropping in. Thank God Louise is back and was over to get her Chrissy fix early this morning." Finally noticing that they were looking across the room, Claire turned to look as well. "Hey, Ava and Brant are here. I better hurry up and deliver this coffee. I think they have a meeting with Jason soon."

Claire now had Beth and Ella's complete attention. "Who are they?" Beth asked.

"Oh, that's Declan's sister, Ava, and his brother, Brant. They own a company that makes one of the components that we use here." Then, lowering her voice, Claire continued. "Jason is interested in buying their company and bringing them on board. They're headquartered near Charlotte, North Carolina."

"Does Declan own part of their company?" Beth asked curiously.

"Yeah, from what I gather, it was left to them by their father when he passed away. Ava and Brant run the day-to-day operations and Declan handles the troubleshooting. It's a very successful business and I know Jason would like to bring it into the Danvers family. Just as we did with Mericom and Gray and Nick, Ava and Brant would relocate to Myrtle Beach and work from the corporate office."

Beth saw Declan looking at Ella inquiringly. "It looks like they've caught us staring; maybe we should go over and introduce ourselves."

"You're right," Claire agreed. "We don't want to take off like we are guilty of talking about them—even though we are."

Ella reluctantly followed them as they walked across the lobby to greet Declan and his family. Claire stepped forward first and graciously offered a hand to each sibling. Beth followed her lead and then all eyes turned to Ella expectantly. Beth could see the slight flush on her friend's cheeks as she squared her shoulders and introduced herself to Ava and Brant. When she came to a stop at Declan, he gave her a soft smile and, if it was possible, she flushed even more.

Again, Beth wondered how Declan felt about Ella. She was sure that Ella had a crush on him. Maybe he was just being nice to her, but something in his eyes made Beth pause. She suspected there was something more than polite friendliness when he looked at Ella. Beth wanted to tell her to start running and never stop because Declan was more than Ella could handle. She needed a nice, dependable guy who would worship the ground she walked on. Declan would shake the very foundation under her, and Beth seriously doubted if Ella would ever recover. Nick might be a bad boy in the ladies' man sense, but Declan was just a bad boy, period.

They all loaded onto the elevator and Claire exited several floors later with the Stone family. *Oh God. Ella just checked out Declan's ass as he left the elevator. I need to have a serious talk with her soon, even if I'm not the best one to give advice. After all, I did get accidentally pregnant with Nick's babies. Maybe I should send Suzy to have a chat with her. It might scare the hell out of Ella, but she wasn't likely to soon forget it.*

Beth parted ways with Ella at the reception desk and continued on to her office. She needed a few moments to come to grips with her doctor's appointment before she had to face Suzy. But just as she finished the thought, the door burst open and her sister strode in. She carefully bit back the groan before it escaped her lips. Suzy perched on the corner of her desk and leaned in closer to Beth.

"So when did you get in?" Suzy asked.

"A few minutes ago. I was just coming to your office," Beth lied.

"So, um, what happened at the baby doctor? Is it in the right place and all?"

Beth smiled at Suzy's obvious discomfort talking about the pregnancy. You would think after Claire's pregnancy that she would be used to it, but she still looked nauseous whenever babies were mentioned. "Yeah, they are just as they should be."

Smiling, Suzy said, "Oh, well, good, glad to hear it." Suddenly her head jerked up and she asked, "They? Shit, please tell me you didn't say that word."

Beth buried her face in her hands and mumbled, "You heard me right. I'm having twins; can you believe it?"

"Holy shit, how did this happen!"

Beth couldn't help but smile at her sister's question. "The usual way, I guess."

Suzy stood up from the corner of the desk and slumped backward in the chair behind her. "My God, what are you doing to do? I mean—*two* babies? Hell, just one freaks me out. I'm not going to babysit, but I will at least pay for a babysitter on a regular basis for you, how about that?"

Beth chuckled. "Thanks, sis. It hasn't really sunk in yet so I don't know what we will do. I just need some time to think."

Suzy jumped up and said, "Hey, I know just what you need: a distraction!"

This can't be good. "What kind of distraction?"

"I need you to help me plan this wedding thingy. Apparently, Gray isn't going to settle for living together forever. He wants to make it official. I told him it would be something simple. I am not walking down the aisle in a church in a gown bigger than I am."

Beth clapped her hands in excitement. This was exactly what she needed to take her mind off her own problems. Of course, Suzy would probably give the term *bridezilla* new meaning, but it sounded like fun. Suddenly, another thought had Beth frowning. *Unless we can pull this wedding together in a month, I'm going to look like a whale. Poor Beth, always a bridesmaid, never a bride.*

While Beth was pondering that depressing thought, Suzy dropped another bombshell. "The parents are coming for dinner Friday night. I told them you would be there."

"What! Have you lost your mind? I can't see them now; they'll know."

"No, they won't. I'm doing you a favor. We'll get the dog-and-pony show out of the way before you start showing and if they decide to skip the wedding, we probably won't see them again until after the babies are born. If it's any consolation to you, Gray is sweating bullets. I tried to tell him that our parents aren't the type to come in and try to defend their little girl's virtue. As long as he has a good IQ, they will be thrilled."

Beth snickered. "How will we know? Their facial expressions never change. If I didn't know better, I would swear they got Botox. So, should I bring Nick with me?"

With an evil smile, Suzy said, "Oh, yeah, he's not getting out of this. Gray probably needs the moral support, too. He thought we should meet them at a restaurant so we could all go our separate ways afterward, but I insisted they come to the house."

Beth had to wonder where her sister's head was. "Did you really think that through? Of course Nick and I can just go home after dinner, but you and Gray will be stuck with them until they decide to leave."

With a grimace, Suzy said, "Shit, I didn't think of that. If I get desperate, I'll have to turn on the television and find one of the comedies. You know how much they hate meaningless shows. I blocked the science channel long ago, so we should be safe."

Beth laughed as Suzy stood to leave. Just as she opened the door, Suzy said, "Hey, I loved the picture of you and Nick passed out on the couch after your night of babysitting. It looked brutal. You guys are in so much trouble—you know that, right?"

Beth flipped one of her sister's favorite hand gestures back at her. Were there no secrets anymore? She didn't think they had done too badly watching Chrissy. No one had to go to the emergency room and they had managed not to panic . . . much. *Suzy is right; we are in trouble.*

*   *   *

Nick sat in his office chair staring out the window. He was proud of how well he had held it together through the doctor's appointment and the drive to work. Now that the shock was wearing off, panic was setting in. *Twins? Dear Lord, what were they going to do? He could think of only one answer to the question. Mom, help! His mother always had an answer for everything and he sincerely hoped she would have some advice on fatherhood.*

With that thought, he remembered the conversation he and his father had had when Gray thought he had fathered a child with Reva. His father had lectured him about safe sex and promised to revisit the conversation if he did something stupid. Now his father would have to break out that lecture again. *How about not one grand-child but two? Oh, yeah, I have been a busy boy.*

He had talked nonstop on the way to the office to fill the silence. He wasn't ready to have an intense conversation with Beth over their future, and he always talked a lot when he was nervous. But now that he was gathering his wits about him, he realized that not much had changed. Sure, there was another baby now, but he was still in it for the long haul. Seeing the heartbeats on the ultrasound had made it feel so real. Beth was carrying his babies inside her. Babies they had created together. He was both scared to death and strangely excited. He was going to be a father, something he had never imagined.

He was jerked from his thoughts when Gray walked

in unannounced and raised an eyebrow at his expression. He imagined he looked like he was in shock. "Everything okay?"

Clearing his throat, Nick said, "Yeah, it's fine. Beth had her first doctor's appointment this morning and, would you believe, we're having twins?"

Gray rocked back on his heels, visibly taken aback by the news. "Damn. I mean congratulations. Wow, that is some news. How are you two handling all of this?"

Nick laughed at his brother's attempt to sound excited. "We haven't had time to talk about it. We came straight to work. I thought I would piss my pants at first, but now I'm down to just the slight urge to pass out. I think Beth is still reeling, too." Then, looking his brother in the eye, he added, "I'm with her, though. She won't do this alone. Those are my babies and I'll never leave them. She might try to force me away, but it's not happening."

"Do you love her?" Gray asked quietly.

"Love? Hell, I don't even know what that is. I care about her. I can't keep my hands off her and I want to be with her. I don't need to label it. It is what it is and I'm happy with that."

"What if that's not enough for Beth? Don't you think she deserves the whole package? Plenty of people raise children that aren't together."

Jumping up from his chair, Nick walked over to his brother, snapping, "What do you know about us? Your romance hasn't been too smooth, either, so I don't think we need any advice from you."

Instead of being mad at his harsh statement, Gray clapped him on the back and smiled. "Good answer. I think you two will be just fine."

Without another word, Gray walked out the door and left him baffled.

It's official, the Merimon brothers have lost their minds.

Chapter Fifteen

Later that day, back at home, Beth shifted around uncomfortably and wondered if she was going to have to resort to "barbecuing alone" as Nick called it. *Why am I so horny?* Even though they had slept together less than twenty-four hours ago, she felt like it had been years. If she had hit one more pothole in the road on the way home, she would have probably had an orgasm from the bump.

As soon as Nick walked in the door, she wrapped herself around him. He probably didn't even know what hit him. He had barely dropped his briefcase on the floor before she was thrusting her hands in his hair and pulling his mouth down to hers. She groaned as the heat of his mouth met hers. You had to give the guy credit; he didn't ask her any questions. Buttons were flying, hands were grabbing and mouths were clinging. She couldn't remember ever being this desperate to have a man inside her. *This* man.

Her hands wrestled with his belt and then the button at the waistband of his slacks. Finally, she had her hand inside his briefs and his erection swelled in her hand. She moaned low in her throat, desperate for his possession.

Nick grabbed the cheeks of her ass and squeezed them while his tongue nipped and sucked at her bottom lip and her tongue. Beth pushed him backward, aiming for the chair, but his feet got tangled in his pants and they ended up in a startled heap on the floor. Her breath left her in a whoosh and she could only imagine how Nick must be faring with the weight of her body pushing against his. As she started to shift to the side, he gripped her hips and whispered softly, "Oh no, baby, finish what you started."

That was all the encouragement she needed. She quickly pushed his briefs down and released his cock to her hungry gaze. Instead of raising herself to lower her panties, she slid them to the side. Circling her hand around his length, she raised herself above him and then lowered onto him slowly, inch by inch. She couldn't remember anything ever feeling better than the slide of his body into hers.

Nick groaned and raised his hips to meet hers. She threw her head back in ecstasy as he caught her newly sensitive breasts in his hands and rubbed the nipples between his thumb and forefinger. She felt a lightning bolt directly to her core as he continued to rub and tweak her nipples almost to the point of pain. With his next tug, she felt her body convulse around his as spasms of pleasure rippled through her body.

His hands moved from her breasts to her ass as he ground into her while she rode the crest of her orgasm. When the ripples subsided, Beth realized that he was still hard inside her. Looking down into his handsome, flushed face, she felt desire start to build in her again. Nick circled his hand around and palmed her mound. One of his fingers slid past her slit and flicked her tightly budded clit. Beth moaned as pleasure coursed anew through her body. She rocked her hips against him trying to rub against his hand while pulling him deeper inside her.

She heard his breathing and shouts grow hoarse as they both strained for release. His fingers were relentless, drawing out a tidal wave of pleasure like she had never known, which washed over her. A scream loud enough to jolt the neighbors ripped from her throat, followed by a shout of release as Nick exploded inside her.

Still joined together, she wilted on top of him as stars continued to dance in front of her eyes. Sweat dripped off them as they gasped for breath.

She felt Nick's chest rumble against her own as he gently played with her hair. "I could get used to this, princess." Then wincing, he continued, "I have something sticking me in the ass that's killing me."

Gently separating from him, she got shakily to her feet so he could roll over. She was horrified when she saw his cell phone lying under him. Nick started laughing when he saw the phone. Grabbing it, he looked at the display and groaned. "Oh no, baby, we butt dialed my mom while you were riding me."

"What? Oh, my God, no!" Beth felt all the blood draining from her face. "Did she answer?"

Nick looked over his phone muttering, "Yeah, looks like the call lasted for a couple of minutes." Giving her a hopeful expression he said, "She probably couldn't hear anything with the phone being under my butt."

Beth cringed as she imagined his mother hearing her yelling, "Oh, Nick, harder, oh yeahhh." She dropped to the couch in mortification. "I can never face your mother now, you know that, right? You will have to take the kids over there by yourself. I'm sure she would rather not have to face the slut that was doing her son while he called her."

Nick laughed, not looking the least bit concerned. "Don't get all worked up over it. I'm sure she had no idea what was going on. Hell, I can't hear half the time on the damn thing when it's directly against my ear." At that moment, his phone rang and he winced. "It's my mother. Just stay quiet and I'll tell her I'm somewhere else."

Beth slumped in a nearby chair, her face flushed with embarrassment. With a smile of reassurance, Nick answered the call. "Hey, Mom, what's up?" He was silent for a moment, apparently listening to her talk. "Oh, sorry about that. I just left the gym. I had my phone in my back pocket and I probably butt dialed you by accident." With an evil grin, he added, "They had the music on pretty loud, that's probably what you heard. A porn flick—I wish. What kind of gym are you going to?" he teased. He changed the subject on that note and Beth breathed a sigh of relief when he ended the call.

"Oh, God, why did you say porn flick?"

Nick chuckled. "She said my gym sounded like the soundtrack of a porn flick." Wiggling his eyebrows he laughed. "That's pretty accurate, huh?" She tossed a pillow at him that landed against the side of his head. Still grinning he said, "Speaking of porn, thanks for the mighty fine welcome home, princess."

She was surprised that she could still blush around him, but she felt her cheeks heat even more. "Blame it on the babies. My hormones are going crazy and you are the lucky beneficiary."

Suddenly looking alarmed he asked, "Should we be doing that? I'm not going to hit them, am I?"

Beth threw back her head and laughed. "Kind of flattering yourself there, aren't you?"

"Ha-ha, you know what I mean. This is safe, right?"

"The doctor said it was fine, remember? Of course, if you want to wait for nine months, I'll understand," she teased.

"If my welcome home was any indication, I don't think you could make it, princess." Rising from the floor, he held a hand out to her, giving her that signature grin she couldn't resist. "Let's go shower off and have dinner. If you're a good girl, I'll let you wash my front."

She could have played hard to get, but why bother? They both knew that she would love to do his front, and she knew he would return the favor. It was a win-win for everyone.

Around four in the morning, she woke up feeling sick once again. Couldn't she have the normal morning sickness that happened after she actually got up? She lay in bed trying to fight off the waves of nausea consuming her. Finally, when she could delay no longer, she jumped from the bed and bolted to her second home: the toilet. She felt Nick's hand on her back soon after and sagged against him weakly. He didn't say anything for a few minutes; he just pulled back her hair and rubbed her back in between bouts.

When she had nothing left inside her, he picked her up as he usually did and sat her on the bathroom counter. She was surprised when he opened a new toothbrush for her. Seeing her questioning look, he said, "I bought you a dozen of these. I know you don't want to use the same toothbrush after being sick."

Beth was surprised at how his small act of kindness moved her. His thinking of something so small touched her more than she could say. She gave him a smile of gratitude and quickly brushed her teeth. He wiped her face with a wet cloth and then carried her back to bed. They had developed a routine in the last week. He supported her while she was sick, cleaned her up, and tucked her back into bed. He then curved his body around hers, gently stroking her until she drifted to sleep. He made the sickness bearable and, during those times, she felt cherished.

When she awoke a few hours later, Nick was already up and drinking a cup of coffee. She quickly showered and walked to her closet to pull out a pair of slacks. When she attempted to button them, something happened that almost stopped her heart: they wouldn't zip. She felt the blood drain from her face as she noticed how tight the pants were. For someone terrified of gaining extra weight back, this was a nightmare come true. Nick walked in the bedroom as she was staring at herself in the mirror. He noticed her look of panic and came to a sudden halt. Alarmed, he took her arm and asked, "Princess, what's wrong? Are you sick again?"

As tears started to roll down her cheeks, she shook her head no. Still looking worried, he asked, "Why are you crying then? Um, is this a hormone thing?" With another shake of her head, she pointed to the opening of her pants.

"I don't have a clue what you are trying to tell me. Do you need me to zip your pants?"

"They won't zip," she wailed. "I can't even pull them all the way together."

A man to the core, Nick said, "Well, just pick another pair. You probably haven't worn those in a while."

The tears flowed harder and Beth gasped out, "I wore them a few weeks ago! I'm barely pregnant and can't wear my clothes anymore. I might as well invest in some big dresses because regular pants aren't going to cover this ass for long."

Stepping up behind her, Nick playfully cupped the cheeks of her butt in his hands before saying, "You have one fine ass, princess, and a few extra pounds isn't going to change that." When she whirled around and threw her hands on her hips, she could tell he knew he had said the wrong thing.

"So now I'm carrying some extra pounds? Well, thanks so much for pointing that out. I thought maybe my body was just changing from the pregnancy, but now, thanks to you, I know that I'm just overweight!"

Nick threw his hands in the air as if trying to ward her off. "Princess . . . I didn't mean it that way. I was just trying to say that you are beautiful no matter what size you are."

"Get out, you big jerk!" Taking off the pants that wouldn't zip, she hit him dead center in the back as he practically ran from the room.

When he reached the door, he risked a quick glance over his shoulder. "Are you riding to the office with me?"

My God, could he be more clueless? Did he honestly think she would get in the car with him this morning after all of his stupid comments? Deep down inside, she knew he had just been trying to make her feel better, but he had seriously botched it. Still, she needed some space. If she rode to work with him, she would probably force him to take her to McDonald's and watch her while she ate her way through the breakfast menu. Luckily, she was saved from replying as he took her silence as no and mumbled that he would see her later.

Returning to her closet in disgust, she pulled on a soft jersey dress, which was both comfortable and flattering. She didn't have the heart to try another pair of slacks. She took a few deep breaths, trying to fight the panic that had been with her since she tried to zip the pants earlier. No one who had never been seriously overweight could understand her paranoia over weight gain. She had worked so hard to get where she was today and being powerless to stop the pounds from piling on was enough to make her feel faint. Maybe she just needed to double her effort to watch what she ate. She wouldn't let pregnancy be a reason to let herself go. She couldn't go back to where she was before—she wouldn't.

Chapter Sixteen

Nick walked into the lobby of Danvers International a few minutes ahead of schedule. He had a conference call at nine, which left him almost an hour to spare. He had been in such a rush to leave home this morning that he had missed breakfast. He was afraid that if he stayed, Beth might stab him with his fork.

He walked over to a private alcove in the spacious lobby and settled on a comfortable sofa. He picked up a copy of *Newsweek* and thumbed through it without reading the pages. His mind went back to the scene with Beth earlier. Could he have messed that one up any more? He couldn't understand why she was so upset over her pants not buttoning. He had been trying to tell her how beautiful she was and damn if he didn't keep sticking his foot in his mouth. What had happened to his magic touch with women? Beth always seemed to keep him off his mark. He could never be "Cool Nick" around her. She turned him into a clumsy schoolboy.

He almost jumped out of his seat when he felt a

hand on his shoulder. "Boy, do I know that look," drawled an amused voice. Nick looked up and cringed at the sympathy in Jason's eyes. He sat in a chair next to the sofa and said, "So, what did you screw up?"

Jerking his head in surprise, Nick asked, "How do you know I screwed something up? Maybe I'm just relaxing for a few minutes."

Jason laughed. "Yeah, right. I've had my ass in the sling too many times not to recognize the look on your face. I imagine I look the same way when I'm in the doghouse."

Grimacing, Nick admitted, "It was about her weight gain."

"Damn. Man, tell me you didn't go there. You never, under any circumstances, admit to a woman, especially a pregnant one, that you think she has gained weight. That's a rookie mistake and I never took you for one."

"No," Nick defended. "I didn't tell her that she had gained weight. She was freaking out because her pants wouldn't button and I tried to reassure her that she would be beautiful at any size. She completely went off the deep end. I thought women dreamed of a man who liked them just the way they are."

Jason chuckled. "What kind of dream world are you in? You should have avoided the whole conversation. I'd have faked an urgent bathroom trip or whatever the hell it took to get me out of there pronto. You can't win those conversations. You said, 'You would look beautiful at any size.' What she actually interpreted from that statement is: 'Yeah, you've gained a lot of weight, but you have such a pretty face.'"

Nick shook his head in disbelief. "No shit? How do you know all of this stuff?"

"I've been there, man. And I have the battle scars to prove it. The first few months of Claire's pregnancy were rough. She was sick all the time and miserable. I kept trying to cheer her up and just ended up making her cry. I refer to it as the first trimester from hell. When I wasn't making her sad, I was pissing her off. She alternated crying on my shoulder and slamming the bedroom door in my face. Finally, one evening she asked me if she had a double chin. Just when I was about to give her what was probably another dumb answer, my cell phone rang and I answered it. By the time the call was finished, she had moved on to something else and I had avoided disaster. From that moment on, I used the distraction technique whenever I could. The Danvers household was back in harmony."

Nick laughed, shaking his head. "That's unbelievable and a lot simpler than the shit storm I created this morning. Thanks for the advice, man; you may well have saved my life."

Gray strolled through the lobby as he and Jason were walking toward the elevator. Nick had to admit, it was hard not to envy the contentment that seemed to radiate from Jason and his brother. It was obvious that they were both happy with their lives, maybe even thrilled.

"Good morning." Giving them a questioning look, Gray asked, "Everything okay?"

With a smirk, Jason said, "Nick took the fat bait this morning."

Gray visibly recoiled. "Tell me you didn't! How could you live with Mom for all of those years and not know any better?"

Nick shook his head in disbelief. "I don't know what is worse here, the fact that you know what Jason is talking about, or having you both laughing at me."

"Hey, I've made that mistake before," Gray admitted. "Both of you know Suzy well, so you know it was a mistake I will never make again. There is only one answer when faced with any questions on weight: no comment. No matter what you have to do to avoid giving an answer, do it. Suzy is still harping on the fact that I agreed that she was too heavy when she was on . . . um, well, never mind when that happened, just heed the warning."

Both he and Jason laughed over Gray's near slip of the tongue. Suzy would probably choke him within an inch of his life if she knew that he had almost spilled on their sex life. As humiliating as it had been to have Jason and Gray laugh at him, he had at least learned a valuable lesson: where women were concerned, less is always more.

Flopping down in a chair in her sister's office, Beth sighed dramatically, "Well, it's official; I'm a fat-ass."

Suzy propped her feet on her desk and crossed one black high-heeled ankle boot over the other. "Come again?"

"I had to resort to wearing a dress today because my pants wouldn't button this morning. Nick kindly told me that I was beautiful no matter how huge I was."

Scowling, Suzy asked, "He said that to you?"

"Something like that. I don't remember his exact words, but he sure didn't have to ask what I was talking about. He even patted me on the butt just to make sure I knew what he was referring to."

"Men are pigs," Suzy snorted. "They just walk around all day flexing their muscles and loving it when we stare at their ass. The sad thing is that it isn't just the hot ones. Even the unattractive, out-of-shape ones still think they are hot. Can you imagine Gray, Nick, and Jason sitting around saying, 'Hey, man, my ass is getting huge' or 'Does this suit make me look fat?' Hell, no, they would never lower themselves to that. Gray looks at me like a deer in the headlights when I ask him anything about my body. It's not like I'm going to kill him or something if he tells me the truth. But he acts like I'm speaking a foreign language." Finally noticing that Beth was laughing, she asked, "What's so funny?"

"I'm still laughing over the mental image of Gray, Nick, and Jason discussing their body insecurities. Instead of asking each other if they look okay, it's more likely that they say stuff like, 'Dude, those jeans make your dick look huge.' They probably meet for lunch at

least once a week to talk about what studs they are."
Beth laughed.

Suzy snickered. "I have taught you well. I think it's
time to set you free and let you fly. Oh, yeah, the parents will be over Saturday at five. . . . I bet that brought
you crashing back down to earth, huh?"

"God, are you really going through with this?
Couldn't you just send them pictures after the wedding?"

"Hey, it's not my fault. Gray has really been putting
the pressure on me. I guess his parents want to meet
my parents. I don't know why. When they get together
and our parents analyze them all evening like a science
project, they will be ready to run for the hills. Of course,
you and Nick making the whole baby announcement
should buy me a few minutes to slip off to the kitchen
and down a bottle of Scotch in between courses."

Beth laughed before her sister's words sank in.
"Wh—what? We aren't making a baby announcement
Saturday night! Are you crazy?"

"Well . . . come on, you might as well get it over
with. I figure we wait until Mom and Dad get into one
of their long speeches on climate change or fossil fuels
and just drop the bomb. During all of the excitement, I
offer to get some champagne from the kitchen. Gray
will go along to give me a hand and we will lean
against the counter on which you had nasty kitchen sex
with Nick and drink until we get enough of a buzz to
survive the rest of the evening."

Beth looked at Suzy in surprise and admiration. "Wow, you have really thought this out, haven't you? You're willing to sacrifice your own sister to make your life easier. I can't even go to the kitchen and drink with you, so what exactly am I getting out of this?"

"It's called taking one for the team—and you are the only one in a position to do it. They already know I'm living in sin with Gray and that we are getting married. They don't know that their sweet little Bethie is living in sin with Gray's brother and that she is knocked up. Come on, just think of the entertainment value here."

Beth shook her head, laughing at Suzy's logic. "So while I am shocking my parents into speechlessness, what are Nick's parents doing? Don't you think they might have some kind of reaction over the news, too?"

"Well, I don't think they will be surprised, do you? I mean it's not like Nick is a choirboy or anything. They probably expected a grandchild from him long before now. I'm sure they will just be thrilled that you aren't paid by the hour or something."

Groaning, Beth said, "You are terrible. If you weren't my sister, I would be terrified of you." As they were both laughing, Claire walked in and plopped in the other seat.

"Ahhh, it's great to see some people that don't need diaper changes."

"Hey, I hope that never happens, but if it does, it's nice to know that you will take care of it," Suzy said, smiling.

Claire turned toward Beth and asked, "So since Nick survived the babysitting the other night, does that mean you're going to give him a chance to do the family thing?"

With a sigh, Beth said, "I don't know. I still feel like he's going to cut and run when things get serious. I just don't know how else to test that theory, short of throwing him out."

"Hmm," Claire said. "Let me think a minute."

"No need to think, I've got it," Suzy announced with an evil smile. "It's time to commence Operation Clinger."

With a wary look, Beth asked, "Operation what?"

"Operation Clinger. It's time to see if Nick can handle having a noose around his neck. So far, Nick has mostly been coming and going as he wants so it's time to give him a glimpse into the future. You may not be a clingy woman, but fatherhood will certainly put some demands on him. Let's give him an early preview and see how he handles it."

Intrigued despite herself, Beth asked, "So how would we do that?"

Claire jumped to her feet in excitement. "You will be the baby or babies, Beth!"

"I will? You two are starting to scare me."

"It's time that you became clingy. All of the freedom he takes for granted needs to suddenly become a lot more difficult. You need to be waiting at the door when he comes home and hanging on his sleeve when he leaves. He shouldn't be able to walk more than a few feet without tripping over you. His swinging single days are over. Let's see if he is ready to say good-bye to them. If he can survive it for even a few weeks without running like hell, then he might be a keeper."

"I . . . I don't know if I can do it. I like my space just as much as he does."

"Well, if you don't think you can pull that off, I can let you babysit Chrissy every evening for a few weeks to see if that does it," Claire offered.

"Um . . . no, that's okay. I think I can do clingy," Beth quickly added.

"Okay, get started tonight and let us know how it goes tomorrow. Boy, I wish I could see his face," Suzy said, and laughed.

Chapter Seventeen

Beth almost laughed aloud when Nick slowly walked through the doorway that evening. He approached her with a wary expression. She had intentionally avoided him all day, knowing it would keep him on edge. Part of her thought she wasn't being fair to him, but then she remembered the babies she was carrying and how devastating it would be for all of them if he decided he didn't want to be involved later on. Nick was a good guy, but sometimes good guys hit the road when things got tough.

In her limited dating experience, each guy she had once hoped might be different had ended up disappointing her. She always thought if she were thin, they would stay, but was that really true? Seeing coworkers' marriages falling apart through the years seemed to indicate that even being slim couldn't make someone stay if they wanted to go. So if they were going to raise a family together she had to know that no matter what, he was going to be here. Maybe she still had issues from her fat days. In her experience, all men left her eventually. She was just somewhere they stopped until something better came along. It would kill her to let Nick into her heart and have him leave her, too. She just couldn't take the risk. She had to know that he was more than a fair-weather man.

Giving Nick her most charming smile, she patted the couch beside her. "Hey, honey, come sit with me. I didn't think you would ever get home." She hid a smile as he looked at her in surprise. The poor man was probably afraid she had forgotten she was pregnant and drank a bottle of wine. As he still looked at her uncertainly, she patted the couch again, saying, "Hurry up, I've missed you." Boy, she must have really been bad this morning if he was so afraid to approach her. He finally walked over and sat beside her.

"Hey, princess. Are you . . . um . . . feeling better?"

Giving him a confused look, she asked, "What do you mean?"

Clearly stumbling now, he quickly said, "Oh, never mind. I just meant I'm glad to see you so happy."

"Ah, thanks." Then giving him her most adoring look, she added, "I ordered Chinese for dinner from that place down the street. I know it's your favorite."

"That's great, princess." He kissed her lightly on the mouth and started to stand. "I'm going to take a shower before dinner if you don't mind. As you can see, I came straight from the gym."

Beth stood up with him. "I don't mind at all. How about I sit in the bathroom with you and we talk about our day?" *Oh, God, look at him squirm. He has rubbed his forehead at least five times since he got home.*

"Don't you need to wait for the delivery guy?"

"Oh, no. I just called before you got home. They only have one driver tonight so it will be at least an hour."

With a shrug of his shoulder, he walked toward the bedroom. Luckily, for an apartment, her bathroom was a good size. He rapidly removed his gym clothes and started the shower. She leaned against the vanity and brightly asked, "So when do you want to look at houses? I thought we could go ahead and start looking. We need some time to move in and decorate the babies' room." She covered a smile with her hand when she heard something hit the shower floor. "Are you okay?"

"Yeah, I just dropped the soap." Clearing his throat, he replied, "So why the sudden change of heart on moving?"

"Oh, I was just being silly. I think we should just go for it. Before long, we will be one big, happy family. You've been trying so hard and it's only fair that I meet you halfway." The shower was quiet as he processed her statement. She looked at the outline of his body in the shower and decided to kick things up a notch. Quickly pulling her clothes off, she opened the back door of the shower and stepped inside. Nick jumped a foot when he turned and saw her standing there. She took the soap from his hands and began washing his breathtaking body without saying a word. She went down on her knees before him, making his eyes widen in surprise.

Nick sucked in a loud breath as she slid the soap down his hips and near his hardening length. "Princess, what—"

His next word was lost in his groan when she took him into her mouth without warning. She gripped his base firmly with her wet hand and started to pump it up and down his length in tempo with her mouth. He fisted his hand in her hair as he pushed his hips against her mouth. When she ran her tongue around the tip of his cock, his whole body jerked. "Shit, Beth, you are gonna be the death of me."

She moved her hand faster and faster, watching his whole body tighten. He suddenly jerked his hips, freeing his cock as he came against the shower wall. She put her hand around his cock and wrung every last bit he had left. Nick might always come in her body, but he always pulled back if he was in her mouth. She had never swallowed before, but she might be willing to try for him. He as always was too considerate to assume that she would.

Nick pulled her against the back of the shower and wrapped his arms around her. She knew from experience that he would recover in a few minutes and would make leisurely love to her. He was in for a surprise, though. Tonight was the start of what she would refer to as cuddling time. She didn't want it to be confused with sex. She kissed him on the chin and untangled herself from his arms. "It's almost time for the delivery guy so I better get dressed." Nick looked baffled. Normally by this point, she would have her legs wrapped around him and be panting for him to come inside her body. She did have the familiar ache between her legs, but she was determined to control herself. Women could go longer without sex than men, right? It was time to see if there was more to their relationship than sex.

Nick was sated, but uneasy. He didn't know what to make of the Beth that had been waiting for him when he came home. He had been prepared to shower her with compliments and make love to her until her toes curled. In his experience, both of those things solved most of his problems with women. He had also stopped at a jewelry store on the way home and bought her a diamond heart pendant just in case the first two things failed to get the desired response. The jewelry box was still in his briefcase because he had been so baffled since arriving home that he truly hadn't remembered it until just now.

Instead of the silent treatment or angry words that he had been expecting, Beth had been sweet and almost loving. He had never seen her act quite like this around him. Their relationship had been built on white-hot sex and the general enjoyment of each other's company. When she walked into a room, he wanted to rip her clothes off and despite her self-esteem issues, she gave her body to him completely and without inhibitions. He was tender with her because he genuinely cared about her and he would never want to hurt her.

When she had been so uncharacteristically affection-ate earlier, it had almost rendered him speechless. He had tried to escape to the shower to regroup but then she had insisted on following him there and talking about buying a house together. He had almost fallen in the shower at her sudden change of heart. Of course, he couldn't complain about what happened next. Beth's beautiful mouth could literally bring him to his knees. He never took pleasure without giving it in return. It was something he prided himself in. He had been shocked when she had pulled away for the first time. She was a constant surprise to him. He had stayed off balance since the moment they met. Just when he thought he had her figured out, she changed just like the wind. He was coming to discover that if he lived a thousand lifetimes, he would never see all of the sides of Beth.

They had loaded the coffee table in the living room with the Chinese food that Beth had ordered. They had taken turns feeding each other with their chopsticks and laughing when more ended up in their laps than in their mouths. Afterward he had settled back onto the couch and pulled her into his arms. He had stroked her already changing stomach softly and marveled at the feelings that coursed through him as he imagined his children already growing inside her. About that time, he had had the urge to run like hell. His heart had started racing and he could feel sweat beading on his forehead. Luckily, Beth couldn't see his face and he focused on keeping his hands steady so that she wouldn't feel them shaking. He worked on slowing his breathing and warding off what was probably the first panic attack that he had ever had.

He was grateful when Beth yawned and he was able to encourage her to go to bed. She insisted that he accompany her and soon they were settled on their sides with her spooned against him. His hand once again rested against her stomach and he felt the stirrings of panic return.

Everything was becoming so real. There really had been no time to think about the repercussions until now. In typical fashion, he had been running full steam ahead since finding out about the pregnancy. He handled stress by making plans, which worked well in business. Now he was faced with the reality of the week ahead. He would meet Beth's parents, who would probably think he was a sleaze for getting their daughter pregnant. He would also tell his own parents, which would carn him a lecture from his father about keeping it in his pants. His mother would probably be thrilled and be buying the babies tiny leather pants.

Why the panic now? Things were going better than expected and Beth seemed to be coming around—so what was the problem all of a sudden? Had he offered her more than he could give? No! He refused to believe that he was one of those people who would try to avoid their responsibilities. These were his children for God's sake and he would be there for them. He would be the kind of father that he was lucky enough to have. He might not have the loving relationship with Beth that his parents had together, but he and Beth could make a good life together with their children. People did it every day. So what if they weren't in love? They cared about each other and had great sex, more than a lot of married couples have. He would do his best to give his children the parents that he had grown up with. Taking another deep breath, he pulled Beth closer and drifted off to sleep.

Chapter Eighteen

Oh, shit, they were coming down the walkway together! Beth looked out the window in Suzy's foyer and saw her parents walking alongside another couple that she assumed were Gray and Nick's parents. She felt butterflies in her stomach as she realized the time of reckoning was close. Despite all her protests, Suzy was still determined that Beth should announce her pregnancy while the parents were here tonight. Nick thought it was a good idea as well. He told her that his parents would be thrilled. She wished that she could say the same about hers.

Gray and Nick came over to her looking unruffled and relaxed. Nick put his hand on the small of her back, offering her a quiet show of support. Suzy flung open the door before the bell rang and she put on her best game face. Her mother and father walked stiffly into the foyer followed by the Merimons.

Beth could see why Suzy liked Gray's mother so much. She was probably a carbon copy of what Suzy would be like in twenty years. They both had the same sense of style and flair. Suzy greeted their own parents with a simple, "Mom, Dad, good to see you." She then turned to Gray's parents and hugged them both with obvious affection. "John and Vicky, I would like for you to meet our parents, Linda and Harris Denton. Mom, Dad, these are Gray and Nick's parents, John and Victoria Merimon."

Her parents extended their hands for a formal handshake from the Merimons. Gray stepped forward next and made the introductions of Nick and himself to Beth and Suzy's parents. Suzy then pulled Beth forward to stand in front of John and Vicky, saying, "I don't believe you have met my sister."

Vicky stepped forward and engulfed Beth into a hug, just as she had Suzy, and John gave her a warm kiss on the cheek. "Beth, we have heard so much about you. It's great to finally meet you in person." Then, turning to Beth's parents, Vicky added, "You must be so proud to have these two lovely young women as daughters." Other than another tight smile, Beth's parents didn't comment on Vicky's statement. All too soon, Beth moved to stand in front of her parents.

Instead of a warm hug from them, her mother asked, "Have there been any new developments in your job search, Beth?"

Why did she always feel like a small child when talking with her parents? She flushed when she noticed all eyes in the room were on her. "Um . . . no. Mom, I'm really not looking for a teaching job right now. I'm enjoying my work at Danvers with Suzy."

Her mother wrinkled her nose in confusion. "Beth, you have a teaching degree. Why would you want to be your sister's secretary? You should at least take this time to continue your education and possibly get your credentials to teach at a higher level. Your goal should be a position where you could achieve academic tenure."

Beth saw Suzy grimace over her mother's shoulder and mouth, "WTF." She was extremely grateful when Suzy followed that by saying loudly, "Dinnertime."

Grateful for the distraction, Beth gave her mother a tight smile and turned to follow her sister to the dining room. Nick leaned down to whisper in her ear, "Damn, you weren't kidding about them were you?"

She nudged him with her elbow, muttering, "Be quiet before they hear you. This can only get worse. Try to stay off their radar or you'll be next."

Gray pulled out a chair for Suzy beside him and then took the seat at the head of the table. Beth and Nick took the seats beside Suzy and their parents. Beth knew that the only thing worse than sitting next to her mother was sitting across from her.

Gray and Suzy had hired a catering company to prepare the meal. The table was laden with smoked turkey and ham, green beans, mashed potatoes, cranberry sauce, and golden rolls. Beth felt her stomach rumble in appreciation; she didn't often have meals like this outside of Thanksgiving or Christmas.

Nick's mother clapped her hands in delight. "This

looks great, I'm starving. Did you two cook this on your own?"

Suzy snorted. "You know me better than that. Your son may be talented in the kitchen, but that's about as far as it goes here. He did make dessert though and I licked the bowl afterward."

Beth braced as she saw her mother shaking her head before adding, "Suzanna has never been a cook so I hope you aren't marrying her expecting that, Grayson. She has always had a whimsical nature as is evidenced by her choice of professions." Beth could see her father nodding his agreement. Her mother might be the more vocal of the two, but her father always agreed with whatever she said.

Gray studied Beth and Suzy's parents and seemed to choose his words carefully. "I don't mind if Suzy never cooks a meal. She gives her heart to everything she does and that is what I love about her." He clasped Suzy's hand in his own and brushed a kiss on her knuckles.

"Aw, thanks, baby," Suzy cooed. Clearly trying to change the subject, she looked at Gray's mother and asked, "So, Vicky, how was your trip to Italy?" Gray's mother took charge of the conversation, telling everyone about their recent anniversary trip.

Beth was grateful to have a few moments of reprieve from further conversation with her parents. Nick reached under the table and rubbed her leg soothingly as if sensing her turmoil. They had barely made it through the first part of dinner and already she wanted to run and hide. It was starting to seem like a really terrible idea to tell everyone about her pregnancy tonight, but she knew Suzy was hoping for the distraction. She, however, didn't think there was any possible way to intentionally make herself a target for more undivided attention. A phone call or a text seemed like a much better way to let them know. All too soon, Vicky was finished telling about their trip, and Beth's father took advantage of the silence to make further, awkward conversation.

"Suzanna, do you and Grayson plan to continue living here after you are married?"

Gray spoke up for both of them. "Please call me Gray, Mr. Denton, and yes, we do intend to make this our home, at least for now."

Beth's father frowned and she could see the wheels turning in his mind. "Gray, you do realize the risks of living this close to the ocean, don't you?" Without giving Gray time to answer, he continued. "The risks of everyday flooding will continue to increase as global warming pushes the sea levels to rise. This whole area could be underwater in the not-so-distant future."

"Dad—" Suzy tried to interject.

"Suzanna, you need to hear this. I know you don't like to think about world events, but the location of your home is very important and this one is a time bomb. You must also think about the biggest risk factor here: hurricanes."

"Myrtle Beach doesn't have many hurricanes," Gray's father offered helpfully.

Not to be deterred, her father leaned forward in his chair and presented his case. "This area does have an active hurricane history. All the way back in 1899, a hurricane called the Halloween Storm made landfall on the North Carolina and South Carolina border, causing extensive damage. Then, in 1906, a severe hurricane hit Myrtle Beach washing away homes and hotels. There were other glancing blows, but Hurricane Hazel in 1954 was one of the most memorable. It made landfall at the highest lunar tide of the year, making it that much worse. Hurricane Hugo in 1989 came ashore as a category four hurricane with up to a twenty-foot storm surge. Imagine living here under those conditions. It's just a matter of time before another catastrophic hurricane such as Hazel and Hugo occurs."

When her father paused to take a breath, Beth blurted out, "I'm pregnant with twins and Nick is the father." She knew she had picked a bad moment to make the announcement when Nick choked a sip of iced tea. She reached over to pat him on the back as he tried to take a breath. She risked a quick look around the table and saw everyone's eyes once again on her. Suzy looked grateful, Gray looked surprised but amused, and both sets of parents seemed to be in a state of shock.

Finally, Suzy jumped up from the table and grabbed Gray's hand. "I think this calls for a celebration. Gray and I will get dessert and a bottle of champagne to celebrate." She dragged a surprised Gray out of the room with her, and Beth had a feeling that they would both be sampling the champagne before bringing it back to the table.

"I thought they had decided against telling the parents about the pregnancy tonight?" Gray asked in confusion.

Pulling a bottle of champagne from the refrigerator, Suzy said, "Don't look a gift horse in the mouth. This probably saved our ass." She handed the bottle to Gray and begged, "Please open this now. I need at least two glasses before I go back in there."

Gray expertly popped the cork and poured two full glasses. "Baby, if I didn't love you so much, I would be running for my life right now. If they start in on sex next, that's probably it for us. I don't think I would ever be able to get it up again."

Suzy leaned back against his muscular chest and chuckled. "God, you have no idea. This is actually good behavior for them. I have seen far worse."

With a look of disbelief, Gray said, "You're kidding. *This* is good behavior. I haven't had a lecture like that since I put a garden snake in my sixth-grade teacher's purse."

Rubbing her bottom against his crotch suggestively, Suzy laughed. "I knew you were a bad boy."

Gray swatted her bottom playfully. "Behave yourself. I'd prefer not to make out on the counter that your sister and my brother christened before us, and I sure can't risk your parents walking in on us. I don't think either one of us would survive that lecture or, God help me, instructions on what we're doing wrong."

"Ugh, please don't say that. I agree on the counter, though. Of course, if Nick and Beth told us everywhere they've made out in this house since they met, we would probably have to burn the place down."

With obvious reluctance, Gray murmured, "We should probably get back in there. Nick and Beth may be in desperate need of our help by now."

Suzy gave him her best pleading look while running the tip of her tongue around her lower lip suggestively. "Aw, do we have to?"

Gray leaned down to capture her mouth in a kiss that curled her toes and sent liquid heat straight to her core. In a husky whisper, Gray said, "I don't think a few more minutes will matter either way." With those words, he wrapped his body around Suzy's and tried to steal a moment of calm in the storm.

At the dining table, John finally spoke to break the silence. "So, congratulations, you two. I had no idea that things were so . . . serious between you."

Vicky jumped up from her chair and came around the table to hug her. "I didn't think I would be a grandmother for quite some time, but I'm so happy for you. How exciting that my boys have fallen in love with sisters." Beth saw the quick look that she shot at Nick as she said the *L* word. Vicky hugged Nick next and then John walked over and hugged her as well.

John then clasped Nick on the shoulder and said, "I think we may have missed a talk or two lately."

Nick smiled up at his father and said, "Maybe one or two. I'm sure you'll make up for them, though."

John laughed. "You've got that right, son."

Beth noticed her parents sat as still as statues on the other side of the table. Clearing her throat, she said, "So, Mom, Dad, big surprise, right?"

Her mother looked at her with disapproval in her eyes. "Yes, Beth, it is a surprise and not something we would have expected from you."

Suzy and Gray entered the dining room just in time to hear her mother's remark. Beth could tell by the slight stiffening of Suzy's shoulders that she knew their mother was actually saying that she would have expected it from Suzy. Gray pulled out a chair for her and then deposited the bottle of champagne on the table. He went back to the kitchen and returned with the strawberry cheesecake he had made.

Beth took the reprieve that the interruption had created and smiled at John and Vicky as they returned to their seats across the table. Suzy asked brightly from the head of the table, "Is everyone ready for dessert?"

Gray cut them all pieces of the cheesecake and Suzy walked around the table delivering the dessert and offering a glass of champagne, a refill of tea, or a cup of coffee. John, Vicky, Gray, and Suzy all opted for the champagne. Suzy and Beth's parents took coffee and, even though Beth knew that Nick wanted the champagne, he took a refill of iced tea just as she did. He was probably afraid that her parents would launch into a lecture on the hazards of alcohol if he indulged.

Beth took a big bite of her cheesecake and closed her eyes in bliss. When she opened them, her mother was staring at her. With a sinking feeling, Beth prepared for what was coming next.

"You do realize that the weight gain from this pregnancy, especially with twins, will be difficult for someone such as yourself?"

Beth could feel the bite that she had taken threaten to come back up as she dropped her head in embarrassment. *Yep, they are all looking at you. Your own mother just pinned the fat cow sign to your forehead for everyone to see. Would it be bad to wish for one of those hurricanes that Dad was harping on earlier? Now would be a good time to be washed away and never have to look at anyone at this table again.*

Beside her, Nick set his fork down with a clatter. He looked her mother squarely in the eyes and softly asked, "What do you mean, by 'someone such as yourself'?"

Beth wanted to crawl under the table and hide. She appreciated his concern, but wanted him to just let it go, rather than make the situation worse. *Now my mother will go into detail about my weight and I'll be humiliated in front of your parents.*

Her father spoke up, obviously missing the edge that had entered Nick's voice. "Beth spent most of her life clinically obese. Instead of taking control of the situation, as we encouraged her to do when she was young, she let it continue into her adult life, increasing her risk of diabetes, high blood pressure, high cholesterol, and coronary artery disease, just to name a few things. As Linda was trying to indicate, a pregnancy for someone with little willpower such as Beth could well cause her relapse into obesity."

Nick shoved his chair back from the table at the same time Suzy slammed her glass down. Beth looked at the usually cool Nick in surprise as he stood up and leaned over the table, looking at both of her parents. "Do you even hear yourselves?" he asked in a deathly quiet voice. Without giving her parents time to reply, he continued. "I am constantly in awe of your daughters. They are smart, funny, intelligent, compassionate, and beautiful. Everyone who knows them loves them. I'm starting to think they must be adopted. I can't imagine you two even having children, much less having two as outstanding as Beth and Suzy."

Beth's father sputtered, "Now, listen here, young man."

"No, you listen here," Nick hissed. "I have always wondered why someone as beautiful and special as Beth would have so many self-esteem issues, and now I know. Have you ever just once praised her or Suzy for anything? Did you actually try to help her eat healthier, or did you just ridicule her for being overweight? Didn't it ever occur to either of you that she might be using food to escape from her life? As my mother will tell you, Gray and I were both heavier when we were young. Not once did our mother insult or criticize us. Instead, we learned to cook our own healthy meals and we took up a lot of hobbies as a family such as biking and swimming. Never did she say we were doing it because we were obese."

Beth wrapped her hand around Nick's arm, trying to calm him down. She had never seen him this upset before. "Nick, it's okay. Really I'm fine."

Nick looked down at her and cupped her face lightly with his hand. His gaze locked on hers and in a softer voice he said, "No, princess, it's not okay." Then, closing his eyes briefly, he murmured, "I can't sit here and let them treat you like this. Are you ready to go?"

She slid her hand into his outstretched palm and let him pull her to her feet. Her mother and father sat across the table staring daggers at both of them. Gray and Suzy stood at the same time. Gray looked around the table and settled his gaze on Beth and Suzy's parents. "Linda, Harris, I completely agree with my brother. Your daughters are two of the most amazing women I have ever had the good fortune to meet, and I ask that you not upset either one of them in my home again."

"Now, see here, Grayson—" Harris began.

"No, sir," Grayson said firmly. "I'm not interested in

continuing this conversation. Out of respect for your daughter, my fiancée, I'm going to let this go without further comment, and I expect you to do the same. There will never be any other remarks in my home that involve any type of negativity concerning Suzy or Beth."

Beth looked over to see that Suzy was suspiciously close to tears. She knew exactly what her sister was feeling. When had they ever had anyone stand up for them? To have the Merimon family defending them now was something that she would never forget. She and Suzy had learned to let their parents vent long ago. Suzy would rebel in some way later, but during a lecture, they just wanted it to be over. Vicky and John had remained quiet through the confrontation and she was surprised and relieved to see the smile of support that they bestowed on her.

Nick clasped Beth's hand and they walked to the head of the table to give Suzy and Gray a hug good-bye. Suzy whispered in her ear, "Same old shit, different day."

Beth hugged her tighter and whispered back, "I didn't think I would make it through a meal without a fat comment."

Nick's mother walked over to embrace Beth, and said, "You take care of those babies. John and I are here for you if you need anything." Vicky hugged Nick next and Beth couldn't hear what she said to him, but she saw his lips curve into a smile. Nick's father hugged them both next and invited them to Charleston for the weekend.

Beth then turned to her parents and gave them a tight smile. "Mom, Dad, it was good to see you again. I hope you have a safe trip home." Her parents gave a polite nod in return and Nick and Beth were soon out the door and walking to Nick's car. Even after the altercation with Nick, she knew her parents would stay until the official end of the evening. They might not say another word, but they would never disregard polite social rules and leave early. She felt sorry for Suzy, Gray, and Nick's parents, who could possibly have to endure another few hours of her parents' company.

Chapter Nineteen

Never had Nick felt more fortunate to have the parents that he did. He'd always thought Beth and Suzy were kidding when they talked about how uptight their parents were. Hell, *uptight* was too good for them. They were downright obnoxious. He couldn't remember one polite word that they had uttered the entire evening. Every word and every eye roll from them was critical. No wonder Beth was so damn terrified to put a bite in her mouth. He could only imagine the criticism that she had endured growing up. It probably wouldn't have mattered if she had been thin; they would still have found something that didn't measure up to their standards. What was surprising was how well she and Suzy had turned out. They could have ended up being cold, uptight clones of their parents instead of the warm, loving people they were. Sure, they both had some quirky personality traits, but that only made them more unique.

Beth hadn't said a word since they had gotten in his car. He had let the silence linger, thinking that she probably needed time to come to terms with the evening. Truthfully, he was a little afraid of what her reaction was going to be. He had told off her parents without even realizing he was about to do it. There was that saying: *I can talk about my family, but no one else can.* He may well have pissed her off and caused a bigger rift between her and her parents. When he had felt Beth shrinking into herself as her mother and father told the entire table about her weight battles, he had just snapped. This beautiful woman was carrying his children and he would not allow anyone to humiliate her in any way, even her own parents.

He could tell that his own parents were appalled as well. When he had hugged his mother, she had whispered in his ear, "My mixing bowls will be waiting for you when you are ready." Almost every decision or heartache he'd had when he was growing up had been talked over in the kitchen. His mother had taught Nick and Gray to cook at an early age, and they both continued to go home when their problems were overwhelming. They both knew that the baking pans, and their mother's and father's listening ears, were always there waiting for them. Damn, he was blessed.

As wonderful and understanding as they were, he knew that his parents had been blindsided with the pregnancy announcement. There would be more questions and more explanations to make there. He didn't really know why he hadn't told them he was practically living with Beth. Maybe because he knew his father would give him "the talk" if he knew that Nick was dating Suzy's baby sister.

Everything had happened so fast between them. It still felt like there had been a whirlwind around him since he first met Beth. They had amazing sex—a lot of it—and then, in the blink of an eye, he was practically living with her. On the rare occasions that he had stopped to ponder it, he had been helpless to pull back. Her vulnerability and insecurities were so at odds with her wild, uninhibited abandon in the bedroom. The women he had dated were usually overconfident and had seduction down to an art form. Beth, on the other hand, would lose herself completely in their lovemaking, giving and taking with equal measure. She would purr with pleasure in his arms as he praised her body. Then, the next morning, when their clothes were on, she turned back into reserved Beth. It was like living with two different women. Maybe that was why the usual boredom had never come. He never knew what to expect from her next and he loved it. He walked around with a near constant hard-on at home, wondering when she would turn back into insatiable Beth.

They arrived at Beth's apartment without either of them saying a word to the other. Nick jogged around and opened the door for her, helping her out of the low-slung car. He entwined his fingers with hers as they made their way up the stairs and into the apartment.

She gave him a tired smile, saying, "I think I'm going to turn in for the night."

"Beth, I'm sorry if I upset you."

Suddenly, she started laughing. "Are you kidding? You were great! I have never seen my parents puckered up that tight before. Thank you for interrupting because their fat talks usually go on for much longer."

Nick felt his relief flow. "So, you're not mad?"

With another snicker, she said, "No way. It was worth all the misery that it will eventually bring. The good news is that they probably won't be inviting us to dinner anytime soon."

With a laugh, he said, "I can live with that. I'm just glad you're okay with it."

Waving her hand, she said, "Yeah, I'm fine." Then with a sigh, she added, "Their delivery method may need some work, but they're right. I'm not like normal pregnant women. I can't use this pregnancy as a reason to let go. I have to be more careful than ever."

Nick felt a ripple of unease as he studied Beth's determined expression. "Princess, you never let go. I don't think you have to worry about it. You barely eat enough to survive on now, and remember, you have to eat extra for the babies now, right?"

"I eat more than enough," she snapped. "The doctor didn't say anything about tripling the amount of my food to feed three people. If I did that, I would gain too much weight. The average weight of a baby when born is around seven pounds so if I gain eighty pounds, how much of it would actually be the babies?"

Nick could tell by her defensive tone that it was time to shut his mouth and end this conversation. Hadn't Jason and Gray warned him to avoid talking about her weight? He was worried though that Beth didn't know when to stop. Was there such a thing as too thin to her anymore? Her parents had scored a direct hit tonight. She may have enjoyed his defense of her, but she quite obviously believed every word they said. But he decided to back off instead of forcing the issue. She had dealt with enough tonight and he knew the stress wasn't good for her.

Giving her a light kiss on the lips, he turned her toward the bedroom and said, "Go ahead and get some sleep, princess. I'm going to unwind some before I go to bed."

With a smile of understanding, Beth said, "I can't imagine why."

How could anyone throw up as much as she had in the last week and still have gained five pounds? Hadn't Suzy, Claire, and Ella tried to warn her against weighing herself on the scales at the mall? Since they had been right there outside the food court, she hadn't been able to resist. She had been so sure she had lost weight. She had been so careful to watch her portion sizes this week and she had been sick every single morning, but still, her ass continued to expand.

Claire looked at her in sympathy. "It's just the water weight gain, Beth. I had the same problem. Sometimes I was too sick to eat anything but crackers for days and I would still gain weight. I kept asking Jason where it was all going, but he never had an answer. Of course, he always had to return a call or something when I was venting so he probably wasn't even listening."

Shaking her head, Suzy said, "He was just avoiding you, Claire. I finally figured out that every time I say anything about my body other than 'do me,' Gray runs as if I've got the plague. I thought he had irritable bowel syndrome or something until I finally figured out that the bathroom is his easiest escape route after a difficult question. It's the one place he is confident I won't follow him." With an evil smile, she added, "I'm thinking about testing my theory and going right in there with him the next time. Of course, if I'm wrong, it will probably be the end of our sex life."

"Ugh," Claire said, and laughed. "I don't think it's worth the risk to find out!"

Ella looked at them all with envy. "I don't know why any of you would ever be worried about your body, you all look great."

"So, Ella," Suzy began, "is there a man on the horizon for you?"

Flushing, Ella mumbled, "Yes, but I can't have him."

All conversation ceased as everyone zeroed in on Ella. "All right, girl, you can't leave us hanging like this. Who is the guy and why can't you have him?" Suzy asked.

Clearly uncomfortable, Ella said, "Just, um . . . never mind."

"Oh hell-to-the-no, Miss Goody Two-shoes, you aren't getting off the hook. You know all of our issues and all about our guys, so let's hear it," Suzy demanded.

Beth wrapped an arm around her friend, giving Suzy and Claire a stern look. "It's okay, Ella; you don't have to say anything." Beth had a pretty good feeling that she knew anyway and didn't think any good could come of Suzy or Claire knowing about Ella's crush on Declan.

"I've got to side with Suzy on this one, Ella," Claire said. "When you're in the girls club, you can't hold back. We might be able to help you."

Suzy pulled Ella over to a seating area in the corner of the mall and, after they were all settled, she said in a surprisingly gentle voice, "Okay, Ella, let's hear it. Claire is right; maybe we can help."

Ella turned an even brighter shade of red as she whispered, "It's Declan."

Suzy and Claire stared at her blankly. "Um, you don't mean our Declan, do you?" Suzy asked.

Nodding her head miserably, Ella said, "Yes, but he treats me like his sister."

With a snort, Suzy said, "Oh, baby, you are way out of your league. How can I explain this? You're like

Nemo swimming around in the ocean without a care in the world and Declan is like the piranha who comes along and eats you without warning."

"Suzy!" Beth shouted.

"What? It's the truth. Declan has been around the block a lot and Ella hasn't taken her training wheels off yet. I know the man is sexy in a dark sort of way, but, sweetie, he would eat you for breakfast and not in a good way." Suzy smirked.

Claire laughed under her breath before she could stop herself. "Ella, I think what Suzy is trying to say is that you don't have much in common with Declan. Jason said that he served a couple of tours in the military. He has probably seen things that most of us never will. He seems haunted, for lack of a better word."

Ella's shoulders slumped in defeat. "I know, but he is so sweet to me. I've mentioned different things that I like to eat and drink a few times and he always shows up with whatever I mentioned a few days later. That means something, right?"

"Wow." Claire sighed. "That is surprising. I can't imagine him doing that. He's always polite, but holds himself apart from everyone else. It's amazing that he talks to you regularly, much less brings you things."

"I think I scared him away," Ella confessed.

Suzy perked up with interest. "Did you make a pass at him?"

Ella flushed again, saying, "No, of course not. I kind of asked him to dinner at my place."

"You little tramp!"

"Suzy!" Beth groaned, clearly horrified.

"I'm kidding, sis. Get your panties out of a wad." Suzy reached over and cuffed Ella on the shoulder with her knuckles. "You go, girl. You're going to make him dinner before you hit on him."

Beth looked on helplessly as Suzy openly laughed. Claire tried to keep a straight face, but snickered at poor Ella. If embarrassment could kill, Ella would be dead on the spot. "All right, everyone, give Ella a break. We are supposed to be helping her, not harassing her." Turning to her friend, she asked gently, "What happened when you asked him for dinner?"

Staring down at her hands, Ella said, "He looked surprised and then he said that he already had plans. I was going to suggest another night, but he said he was late for a meeting and took off. That was days ago, and I haven't seen him since then. I . . . I think he's avoiding me now."

"Ah, come on now, Ella, maybe he's out of town. He travels a lot, doesn't he?" Beth asked.

Everyone looked at Claire since she usually knew when any of the main group was out of town. Claire gave a grimace and said, "No, I know Declan is in the office this week because he's been working on a contract with Jason."

Shaking her head in disgust, Suzy said, "I'm not going to soft-pedal this to you, Ella; he is avoiding you. He's been sniffing around your feet, but when you started sniffing back, he packed his toys and went home. To someone like Declan you must seem like the ultimate forbidden fruit. He's probably used to women he can screw and then slip out before they wake up. Most of his women have probably been ridden hard and put up wet."

Claire started laughing. "Where do you come up with this stuff?" Then, turning to Ella, she said, "I think what Suzy means is that Declan has a lot more experience than you and maybe he is afraid of hurting you."

"Oh, come on." Suzy snorted. "Ella doesn't need everything I say explained to her. She knows what I'm talking about. Okay, give me a few days to think on this one. I'm sure we can come up with a plan for you to land Declan if you really want to. Look at Beth; she landed her man through wild sex on my kitchen counters and all over my damn house. I'm sure I can come up with something for you. Maybe Claire could loan you her house, though. I don't think I can stomach any more naked bodies sliding across my granite countertops."

When everyone got their laughter under control, Suzy added, "We're going to have a barbecue on Saturday to rid our house of the evil from our last dinner party. I promise that my parents will not be there so you don't have to make excuses." Wiggling her eyebrows at Ella, she said, "I promise that Gray will make sure Declan is there so wear something hot. Oh, crap, never mind, I don't trust you to know what that is, so let's go pick out something for you right now."

"Hey," Beth said, "I thought we were going to look at wedding dresses for you and make some plans?"

"Nah, we can do that next week. Ella is our priority now."

Beth couldn't help but chuckle at Ella's terrified expression. Putting her arm around her friend, Beth whispered in her ear, "Just go with it. If you argue, it will get more painful. It's better to give in now because you can't win."

Chapter Twenty

Beth stood in front of her bedroom mirror studying her body. She had tried to laugh off the scales in front of the girls at the mall today, but the number still stung. It had to be the late dinners with Nick, because otherwise she thought she had been eating really well lately. Since he usually stopped at the gym on the way home, it was usually around seven before they ate. Maybe she could start skipping dinner completely. She could just tell Nick that she was too hungry to wait, and he would never know the difference. He had been making comments on her small portions lately and she didn't want him to know that she planned to miss a meal. It was unreal how when you're fat the world seems interested in every bite you put in your mouth, and when you lose the weight, they still seem just as interested.

First, her parents wanted to make sure she didn't eat too much and blow up, and Nick wanted to make sure she ate enough. Would there ever be a time in her life when no one gave a damn what she ate? Why couldn't she enjoy her pregnancy like other new first-time mothers-to-be?

She was excited and nervous about being a mother. When she could rise above the panic of gaining weight, she thought a lot about the type of mother she wanted to be. One thing she was certain of, she would never be as cold and distant as her mother. Her children would be allowed to have dreams and they would have the childhood that Suzy and she had always dreamed of.

She heard the door slam in the other room and she quickly stepped away from the mirror. It wouldn't do for Nick to think that she was worrying about her weight. She didn't want him to be suspicious when he didn't see her eating.

Beth walked back into the living room as Nick tossed his keys on the table and dropped his gym bag on the floor. She could feel her heart kick into gear as her eyes slid hungrily over his body. Athletic shorts hung low on his lean hips and narrow waist. His biceps glistened with sweat and his tank top outlined his muscular chest. *Oh, girl, you are in trouble. There is no way you can settle for cuddling again tonight with that sitting next to you. When did you become obsessed with sweaty guys? Shouldn't you want him to shower first?*

Cocking a brow at her, Nick asked, "Hey, princess, what do you want for dinner?"

"You," Beth moaned. "I mean . . ."

With a grin, he asked, "Could you be a little more specific?"

Beth walked over to him and slid a hand across one of his hard butt cheeks, giving it a firm squeeze. "Is that specific enough for you?"

Giving her a sexy grin, he said, "I'm still not clear on your meaning."

"Hmm, well, let me make myself a little clearer for you." Leaving one hand on his ass, she brought her other hand in front and found him rock hard against the flimsy material of his shorts. She traced her hand up his shaft, gripping him firmly. "Get the picture now?"

Heat blazed in his eyes as he pushed himself against her hand. "Oh, yeah, I've got it, baby, and I would be more than happy to give it to you."

Nick lifted her suddenly and laid her on the table, knocking his keys to the floor. He jerked up her skirt to her waist and, through her panties, he cupped his hand over her mound. Feeling the moisture on the fabric, he gave her a rakish grin. "Someone has been waiting for me to get home."

Beth could only moan as he continued to caress her through the fabric. She bucked her hips against him, wanting his fingers on her bare flesh, but he continued to deny her. He stroked along her slit, edging the panty-covered tip of one finger inside her. Beth groaned deeper in frustration. He only chuckled. Then, frustrating her even more, his hand left her completely and wandered up to unbutton her blouse. He pulled her bra down and her breasts spilled from the top of the cups.

He moved in tighter between her legs, rubbing his erection against her core as he took one puckered nipple inside his mouth and nipped it lightly with his teeth. Pain and pleasure converged as his teeth and tongue worked her nipples. Each tug on their sensitive peaks caused an answering surge of heat to blaze through her sex.

He lowered his head to her ear and ran the tip of his tongue around the shell. Then he whispered, "Is this what you had in mind?"

"Oh, God, yes," she moaned. She locked her legs around his waist and bucked against his cock. "Now, Nick, stop teasing me!"

The teasing light was gone from his eyes as the friction of their bodies rubbing together finally pushed him into the same frantic mode that she was in. He pulled back enough to lower his shorts and briefs. His erection sprang forward in all of its glory. Beth could feel her body moisten further in anticipation. He pulled her legs loose and raised them into the air. He slid her panties off quickly and lowered her legs over his shoulders. Her bottom was elevated in the air as he positioned his large cock at her entrance. He rubbed the head back and forth, lubricating himself with her moisture. "Oh, princess, you are so wet." Without warning, he plunged forward and buried his cock deep inside her.

"Agh! Oh, that feels so good," Beth shouted. He set a fast, relentless pace. The sound of their bodies slapping together as she rose to meet his thrusts filled the room. She felt like she would explode if she didn't reach the peak that she was driving toward. Without warning, he pulled out of her body and flipped her over onto her knees. As she started to protest the loss of his heat, he slammed back into her from behind. Her head fell forward as he drove deeper than she'd ever thought possible. He grabbed her hips as his cock surged into her again and again. Just when she thought she couldn't take the unbearable ache any longer, she felt his fingers between her slick folds rubbing against her sensitive clit. Stars exploded behind her eyes as the first waves of her orgasm started to rush through her. Her body clenched around his cock, seeming to pull him deeper inside her.

From behind her, she heard Nick's hoarse shout as his powerful body started to jerk. Her orgasm seemed to set off his and soon they were both moaning and shaking in ecstasy. She felt him rest his forehead on her back as he fought to regain control. "Shit," he muttered shakily. "That was freaking off the charts, princess."

A tired laugh escaped her at his statement. "Not too shabby, Mr. Merimon. All of that working out that you do is really paying off. If all the guys at the gym have that much stamina, I might have to start spending more time there."

Nick playfully swatted her exposed behind. "Ha-ha. I think I can take care of everything you need. Now, let's go shower off and have dinner."

Beth tried to look nonchalant as they walked toward the bathroom. "The shower sounds good, but I've already eaten."

"Really? What did you have? Are there any leftovers for me?"

"Um, no. I just made a sandwich when I got home. I think I'm going to start eating earlier. Maybe these late meals are causing me to get sick in the night."

"Hmm, well, maybe. I'll start grabbing something before I hit the gym, then. I usually just wait so we can eat together, but if you think it will help you to eat earlier, then you should."

Beth couldn't help but feel guilty when he admitted that he waited to eat with her. What else could she do, though? No one understood the struggle she faced every day. Those who knew her when she was heavy were just waiting for her to fail, and those who only knew the thin Beth couldn't understand why she was so careful about what she ate. If she let it happen, she could gain a huge amount of weight with her pregnancy and, after the babies were born, she would never go back to the way she was now. All of her hard work would be over and Nick would be gone. No way would someone like him stay with the person she had been.

There was no one she could talk to. She would eat small amounts when people were around, but when she was alone, she wouldn't eat. She would drink a lot of water instead to feel full. Surely, that would slow down the weight gain. If the babies averaged seven or less pounds at their birth, there was no reason that she had to gain more than fifteen or twenty pounds at the most. Everyone would be impressed at how soon she was back to her normal weight after the babies were born.

She walked into the bathroom just as Nick was stepping out of the shower. "Hey, slowpoke, what took you so long?" he asked.

With a chuckle, she said, "I was just taking a break. For some reason, I'm completely worn out. Oh, by the way, Suzy and Gray are having a barbecue Saturday night."

Nick swung around to look at her. "Please tell me your parents aren't going to be there. I don't think I can stomach that two weekends in a row." Then, lowering his voice in a perfect imitation of her father's, he said, "Oh, Gray, you better move before a huge cyclone hits your house and knocks the blocks right out from under it. Suzy, where did you get that trampy-looking shirt that you're wearing? It looks like a sheer tablecloth. Beth, how could you get with child? You know we raised you to believe that people should never, ever have sex. You mother and I conceived you in a test tube on our lunch break."

Beth fell against the counter, laughing hysterically. "God, please stop! I'm going to pee my pants if you don't shut up and leave this bathroom now!"

They continued to laugh, but Nick took the threat seriously and made a hasty retreat. Suddenly, the door opened again and he had a questioning look on his handsome face. Shaking her head, she said, "No, they aren't coming."

Giving her a devilish grin, he said, "Sweet!" and slammed the door.

The remainder of the week passed in a blur of work and sex. How had she ever believed she could deny herself the pleasure of sex with Nick? If the man had one specialty, it had to be in the bedroom—or the kitchen, living room, bathroom, hell, pretty much everywhere. She couldn't seem to get enough of him.

He was also on his best behavior outside the bedroom. As she continued to get sick almost every morning, he was right there holding her hair back, and cleaning her up after it was over. They had also settled into a new routine for their meals. He ate most days before he got home and she continued to let him think that she was eating earlier. The few times he had brought her something sweet, she had nibbled on it until she could discreetly throw it away. Her new diligence seemed to be paying off because she had actually been down a pound that morning for the first time.

Even though her weight seemed to have stabilized, her clothes were still getting tighter and tighter. She was wearing more dresses because the waistbands of her slacks were no longer buttoning. She had resorted to holding the last pair that she had worn to the office together with a rubber band. Due to her pregnancy she could now see the faint outline of a tummy that hadn't been there a month ago. She was waiting for Nick to say something stupid like "More woman to love." If he did, she would probably sit down and cry for an hour since her hormones were out of control. Luckily, he seemed to have good self-preservation instincts and had been unusually sweet and supportive.

Nick's mother had called her yesterday and they had talked for a long time. She was so different from her own mother. If Beth combined all of her phone conversations with her mother in the last ten years, they probably wouldn't add up to the length of this one call with Nick's mom. Vicky was so funny and excited about the baby, and she didn't mention Beth's relationship with Nick or ask if they were getting married at all. Vicky wanted to give her a baby shower when she was further along because, as she put it, "We have a lot of friends with money who love nothing better than to spend it." Vicky also made it clear that she and Nick's father were completely supportive and were there if she and Nick needed anything. Beth had promised that they would go to Charleston for a weekend soon to spend some time with his parents. She had a feeling that she was going to like them immensely.

Beth decided she should probably start lining up replacement parents anyway because her own weren't likely to ever speak to her again. Vicky and John were going to be at Gray and Suzy's this evening and Beth was looking forward to spending some time with them without her own parents ruining the evening.

Chapter Twenty-one

Suzy was nowhere to be seen when Beth and Nick arrived for the barbecue. Gray answered the door and ushered them into the living room. Due to a last-minute "meeting" with Nick on the sofa, they were the last ones to arrive. Nick's mother and father hugged her warmly and then Nick and Beth walked over to talk with Jason, Declan, and Claire.

"Well, Declan and Ella are both here, but things look a bit tense," Claire whispered.

Nick was talking to Jason and Declan and Beth motioned Ella over to where she was standing with Claire. "I love the dress we picked out. You look wonderful."

Blushing with pleasure at the compliment, Ella said, "Thanks, but I don't think anyone else has noticed."

"Oh, I think he noticed all right. I just saw him checking you out," Claire said. "Just play it casual and let him come to you. I'm betting that before the evening is over he won't be able to resist at least talking to you. He might not drag you behind a bush, but conversation is a starting point, right?"

Beth looked around the room and asked, "Where is Suzy? We know she isn't in the kitchen cooking."

Shrugging her shoulders, Claire said, "I don't know. She's usually the center of attention. I asked Gray and he just said that she had a few calls to return."

"That's weird. I don't know of anything major that we have going on at work so I can't imagine what it could be," Beth replied.

At the other side of the room Nick clapped his brother on the shoulder and asked, "So, are we eating tonight? If not, you might want to pass the drink tray around."

Gray laughed. "Yeah, I'm just waiting for Suzy."

Beth had to admit that Gray looked the best she had ever seen him. Contentment seemed to radiate from him. It was obvious that he was very happy with Suzy. All was right in their world, and Beth couldn't think of anyone who deserved it more than her sister.

Suddenly, Gray looked at his watch and cleared his throat. "Okay, everyone, why don't we head outside. We decided to do something a little different this evening, so we set up everything on the beach in back of the house. It's a mild evening, so we might as well enjoy it. Suzy will meet us there when she's ready."

Does anyone else think this is weird? If I didn't know Gray better, I'd be in the kitchen checking the freezer for Suzy's body. What could possibly be keeping her from being here with everyone? Was she even at home? Maybe she'd had a fight with Gray before the party. But if that were so, surely Gray wouldn't look so happy.

Beth was glad to know that it wasn't just her when Claire leaned over and asked, "Does this seem a little strange to you?"

"Yeah, it sure does. But you know Suzy. It could be anything. Maybe her leather pants had a run and she's in the bathroom cussing up a blue streak."

Claire chuckled as they walked onto the patio and started down the stairs. When they turned the corner, and the beach came into sight, everyone froze. Beth heard Nick mutter, "Either someone's getting baptized or married."

"Oh, my," Claire breathed. "They're getting married! I can't believe it. Hey, she picked out a dress without us."

Everyone slowly made their way forward. Beth could see tears rolling down Gray's mother's cheeks as she clasped her husband's hand tightly.

Suzy stood next to a white arbor with white tulle woven through it. She was simply breathtaking. Her long red hair was loose and the wind made it look like a halo around her. She was wearing a white lace gown with spaghetti straps and a sweetheart neckline. A long train flowed behind the fitted dress and the detailed beadwork glistened in the early evening sunset. Beth smiled as she saw Suzy's bare feet peeping from beneath the hem of the dress. She had never seen her beautiful sister more radiant.

A man whom Beth didn't recognize stood beside Suzy, smiling as they all came forward.

"Since Suzy and I have never done anything in our relationship in the normal way, why start now?" Gray said, and laughed. "You are our dearest friends and family and we want to share this moment with you and no one else. Suzy's parents had a previous engagement and we regret that they couldn't be here to round out the circle."

Nick choked. "I can't believe he got that last part out with a straight face."

Beth elbowed him in the ribs and continued to listen to Gray. "We apologize that we sprung this on you, but I think you know that Suzy loves surprises and, truthfully, I love her and this idea. I hope that the men in the group will be my unofficial groomsmen, and I know Suzy wants the women to be her bridesmaids."

Beth ran forward and gave her sister a hug. "I'm going to kill you for not telling me."

"Me, too," Claire chimed in. "How could you deny us the torture . . . um, I mean pleasure of planning your wedding?"

Ella stepped forward and gave Suzy a tentative hug next. "You look so beautiful. Your dress is so—"

"Not me?" Suzy asked.

Ella stammered, "No, I mean, it's just so . . . soft."

Claire stepped in to bail out Ella. "I believe Ella means that the dress is different from your usual style, but I love it. You make a beautiful bride and I'm so happy for you."

Suzy did a twirl in the dress, saying, "I don't know why, but I loved this dress as soon as I saw it. I wanted to look different for my wedding day and this is drastic for me. Ella was right, the dress is soft and that's why I liked it so much. Gray makes me a softer version of myself, so it's fitting."

Gray's parents stepped forward to hug Suzy, and they all lined up for the informal ceremony.

Mr. Maxwell, the justice of the peace and the man Beth hadn't recognized, had agreed to perform the private ceremony. He started with the standard wedding passages, and then said, "Grayson and Suzanna have written their own vows and will be exchanging them now."

Suzy looked into Gray's eyes while holding on to his hands and said, "I, Suzanna Denton, take thee, Gray son Merimon, to be my lawfully wedded husband. I promise that from this day forward, your life will never be predictable or boring. I promise to limit our family dinners and rescue you anytime my parents have you cornered, and I promise to tell you when you are being uptight, and forgive you when you apologize. You are every fairy tale that I dreamed of and the forever after that I never dared to hope for. My heart is finally at home with yours, and it will remain there as long as we both shall live and into the beyond."

Gray brushed a tear from Suzy's cheek with his thumb as he looked into her eyes. "I, Grayson Merimon, take thee, Suzanna Denton, to be my lawfully wedded wife. I promise never to use starch in my underwear again. I promise to attend all the Gamecock football games with you, and I promise to learn all of the words to every Bon Jovi song. You are my soul mate, the love of my life, and the woman of my dreams. Never will there be another woman for me. Our hearts and our paths will forever be intertwined."

Beth sobbed quietly as she watched her sister marry the man of her dreams and was relieved to feel Nick gently slip in behind her and pull her back into his arms. "Shhh, it's okay, princess," he whispered into her ear as his lips gently grazed her neck.

When the couple were pronounced husband and wife, Gray swept Suzy into his arms in an elaborate dip and kissed her until Mr. Maxwell cleared his throat and said, "I am pleased to present Mr. and Mrs. Grayson Merimon. May every happiness in life be bestowed upon your union."

Tears and hugs flowed freely as everyone rushed to congratulate the happy couple. Beth threw her arms around her sister, whispering in her ear, "I'm so happy for you, sis, and I'm sorry that Mom and Dad didn't come."

Suzy looked at her with a smile. "Hey, it doesn't matter. If we had parents like Gray's, then I would have been upset, but our parents would have ruined the day and you know it. Besides," she joked, "they gave me some funny lines for my vows, so it's all good."

Leave it to Suzy to see the bright side of anything. Gray had mellowed her wild-child sister and it was amazing. She was still the same outspoken, edgy person, but Gray had softened those edges to where they were no longer razor sharp. He had finally shown her the unconditional love that Beth had come to think was a myth. Looking at them now, so deeply in love and so at peace with each other, caused a pang of emptiness in Beth's heart. Would that ever happen to her? Her relationship with Nick was both exciting and comfortable, but would it ever grow to be love?

Nick made it a point to be the first in line to kiss the bride at any wedding he attended, but the bride's sister beat him today. But if he had to lose, then who better to prevail over him? Beth's eyes were still misty from the ceremony. She was a lot more emotional these days than when they had first met. He found that he secretly liked this softer side she had started to show him. She had never been jarring like Suzy, but she could cut you off at the knees when she wanted to.

Nick still worried about the situation with her parents. There had been no contact since he had blown up at them at the last dinner, and although he didn't miss them, he wasn't so sure about Beth. She usually changed the subject when he brought them up. She assured him that she wasn't bothered by their ugly words about her, but he wasn't sure about that. Her eating habits had changed since then and he suspected that her parents were the reason. He never saw her eat anymore. She seemed to avoid meals with him altogether, and the few times they did eat together, he couldn't recall anything actually going in her mouth.

Maybe he was worrying over nothing. Her parents may have made her too self-conscious to eat in front of him now, which was a damn shame. She said she was just trying to lessen her morning sickness and he hoped that was all it was, although something about it gave him a feeling of unease. This was a tough time for a woman and she probably needed more support and compliments from him. He could definitely step things up in that area. He would ask Suzy to keep an eye on her as well. There was no way he was going to allow the poisonous words of her parents to shed a single doubt on what a beautiful woman she was.

The women finally had a moment to themselves. A catering service had arrived a few moments after the wedding and, by the time they reached the patio, a buffet and tables had been set up for the guests. Beth wanted to groan when she saw the array of mouth-watering food.

She loaded a small plate with a piece of fish and some green beans. Beside her, Suzy was on her second plate of food. Oh, how she envied her sister's ability to eat anything and never worry about it.

Like Beth, Ella seemed barely to be nibbling at her food, but for altogether different reasons. Declan had yet to seek her out and she was starting to despair that it would ever happen. Beth hated to think it, but maybe it was for the best. She didn't like imagining how badly he could hurt her friend, if given the chance. Ella was a very special person but Beth still felt like she would be out of her league with someone as worldly wise as Declan. He wasn't the right man for her.

"So I made sure Gray got Declan here just for you, Ella. I made a special effort, despite all the wedding planning, to get that man here, and you're still sitting in the corner. You're wearing the dress and he's looked at the merchandise, so what the hell are you waiting on, an engraved invitation?" Suzy asked.

"Every time I get near him, he goes the other way. I don't know what else to do. He doesn't want anything to do with me and I might as well accept it."

"Oh, horseshit! Do I have to do everything around here? I'm going to set up some dancing and you are going to dance with him. Leave the details to me. I will make sure it happens. You just push those girls up there in his face and give it all you've got."

Claire burst out laughing. "Only you could be at your own wedding, Suzy, and be trying to hook up your friend. Shouldn't you be basking in the moment with your groom and not worrying about Ella's girls being on display?"

"It might be my wedding, but when someone is so

obviously in need of my expert services, I can't turn them away. Just hang on, Ella, and I'll take care of it as soon as we cut that big-ass cake that Gray ordered. There are only a few of us; what does he think we're going to do with the rest of it?"

"Hey, Beth," Claire said. "How are things working out with Operation Clinger? Has Nick resorted to begging yet?"

Beth turned a shade of red usually reserved for Ella. "Um . . . I couldn't make it past the second day. I don't know what's wrong with me, but I want sex all the time. I don't want to cuddle with him; I want to jump his bones . . . all the time."

"Ugh," Suzy interjected. "That's wrong. Shouldn't you be nesting or something and not doing our boss nine ways 'til Sunday?"

"I knew you would never make it." Claire laughed. "I was the same way when I was pregnant. Jason refers to it as the glory days. I didn't even need him around to get off."

Looking from Claire to Beth, Suzy asked, "When did you both turn into me? If Ella suddenly starts talking about sex and orgasms, I will know the world is on the verge of collapse."

Suddenly, Beth had a thought. "Hey, where are you two going on your honeymoon? Since we didn't know anything about the wedding, I think we at least deserve to know where you're going ahead of time."

"Well, I really hate to admit this, but I don't know.

Gray wanted to surprise me. I just hope it doesn't horrify me instead. It had better not be some hiking trip somewhere. I like to chill in my downtime and put forth very little effort." Then, giving a saucy grin, she added, "Well, unless it's between the sheets, and then it's my pleasure."

Beth and Claire laughed and Ella turned her usual shade of crimson, but gave a shy smile. The poor girl would probably be high-fiving them soon if she continued to spend so much time around Suzy.

Gray walked over at that moment and leaned down to kiss Suzy on the top of her head. "I don't even want to know what you three are laughing about. I think it's time for our dance, Mrs. Merimon." Suzy took the hand that Gray extended and pulled him aside. Beth saw Gray shake his head and give her an indulgent smile. They walked to the center of the patio and Gray said, "Excuse me for a moment, everyone." When all eyes were on him, he continued. "As you all know, my wife is very shy and doesn't like to be the center of attention." As the hoots of laughter finally died down, Gray continued. "Since my wife is so shy, we would both love it if everyone would join us in our first dance as a married couple. So Mom and Dad, Jason and Claire, Nick and Beth, and Declan and Ella, we would consider this the perfect wedding if you would join in as well."

"Oh, brother," Claire murmured. "That girl is evil and she even has Gray in on the action. All right, Ella, don't just stare at him, get up and make your move. Suzy probably had to promise Gray something illegal tonight in order to pull this off for you."

"What if he doesn't want to dance with me?" Ella asked timidly.

"Trust me, Ella," Beth added, "he does. I caught him staring at you at least a dozen times tonight, so go for it. Give him a chance to see or feel what he's missing."

Beth smiled as the opening notes of a song from one of her sister's favorite bands started up. "Thank You for Loving Me," by Bon Jovi began to play as Suzy and Gray wrapped their arms around each other. Nick pulled Beth from her chair and swung her into his arms, joining his parents who were obviously experienced dancers. Claire and Jason followed them, leaving only one couple who had yet to join the dancing. Beth looked over her shoulder to see Declan offer his hand to a shy Ella. She could see the beaming smile that Ella bestowed on Declan as he too pulled her onto the patio's informal dance floor.

"My sister is an evil genius," Beth whispered into Nick's ear.

Nick looked at her in question. "Other than the usual things, is there any particular reason for you to say that tonight?"

Beth cut her eyes to Declan and Ella. Nick looked, and understanding came into his eyes. "Those two? Are you kidding me? Your sister has missed her mark;

they have, like, zero in common. I like Declan, but he is . . . way out of her league."

"I know," she admitted. "But she really likes him, and he seems to feel something for her. Have you ever known him to have casual conversations with anyone?"

"Nope," Nick said. "He's direct and blunt."

"See, that's just it. He isn't like that with her. He seeks her out. He brings her things and it just seems like he's different with her. I have seen it with my own two eyes or I wouldn't believe it. She asked him over for dinner last week and he's been avoiding her ever since." With a sigh, Beth shrugged. "Maybe he just sees her like a sister."

Nick chuckled. "I've met his sister and he isn't all warm and fuzzy with her. I can't imagine he ever was." He glanced over at Ella and added, "She's very pretty and it looks like he knows that. Maybe he's trying to do the right thing and not bring his shitload of baggage to her. He's been to some bad places in life and it would probably scare Snow White to death if she had seen half of what he has. I think Suzy should leave this one alone, and if Ella is your best friend, then you should tell her to find another guy to wear her heart on her sleeve for. Declan might try not to, but he will crush her."

Beth followed his gaze and studied the two of them together. Ella looked up at Declan in adoration and he looked down at her with an expression that was clearly torn and conflicted. It was plain to see that he felt something for Ella. Beth had a feeling that Nick was right, and that if she were any kind of friend, she should tell Ella to run and never look back. The bad thing was that Ella probably wouldn't listen. Maybe at some point in every woman's life she has to have her heart broken by a bad boy so she can appreciate the good ones when they came along. Looking up at Nick, Beth had to wonder if he was a bad boy or a good guy. She had always assumed he fit neatly into the bad-boy column, but now she wasn't so sure. Nick had some of the same traits, but deep down she knew he was a good man. Was that also true of Declan, or was he past saving? She also knew that if anyone could save him, Ella could.

The party lasted until well into the morning, when Suzy finally stood up in front of everyone and said, "Don't you people know when to go home? It's my wedding night, and if you would pack it up and leave, I would make my new groom a very happy man."

Gray stepped forward smoothly and curled his arm around Suzy. "Your new groom is already a very happy man, but I like where you're going with this."

Clearing her throat, an emotional Suzy said, "On a serious note, I want to thank you for being here on the happiest day of my life. I know I bust your chops on a regular basis, but I love you all and this has been the perfect night for me because the most important people in my world are here." With a very un-Suzy-like sniff, she whispered, "I love you guys to the moon and back."

Gray pulled her deeper into his arms and kissed her tenderly in front of all their guests. Then, with misty eyes of his own, he said, "I agree with Suzy. Each of you here is now family to us. No one here should ever doubt our dedication to each other or to each of you. We hope this is always somewhere you call home." With a cough, he looked at Nick and added, "We would be happy if some of you didn't make yourself so much at home."

Embarrassed, Beth turned her face into Nick's side and said, "He is never going to get over that whole sex-in-his-house thing, is he?"

Nick's body shook in laughter. "Nope. When you decided to confess to your sister, you should have told her we had sex at a Howard Johnson or something. Did you have to specifically mention the kitchen counter?"

"Yeah, my bad." Beth laughed.

Then everyone said good-bye to the newlyweds, and Vicky pulled Beth away from Nick, tucking Beth's arm through hers. "We are so happy to have our families officially joined now. John and I couldn't love Suzy more if she were our own daughter." Then, with a laugh, she admitted, "I would love to raid her closet. Your sister and I seem to have the same taste in clothing."

Beth smiled, enjoying the easy conversation with

Nick's mother. "Yes, I've always admired Suzy's unique style. No matter what she wears, she looks great. I could never pull off stuff like she does."

"Are you kidding? Beth, you are gorgeous, and a paper sack would look good on you. I really admire you. I don't think anything in your life has come easy, and look at you today. You have accomplished so much. I can see why Nick is attracted to you." Then, with a sly laugh, she added, "We won't mention the obvious reasons that you turn his head. I have a feeling that you could give my son a run for his money any day of the week and he needs that. I don't know your plans for the future or even if you and Nick have discussed them, but John and I look forward to you and the babies being a big part of our life always."

Beth was starting to tear up when Nick and his father walked up. His father pulled her into a warm hug and then put his arm around his wife. "Honey, we need to go. You know my parents will be in first thing tomorrow and we probably both need some sleep for that."

With a dramatic shudder, Nick's mother said, "Great, thanks for ruining a perfectly good evening with that reminder." Turning to Nick and Beth, she said, "Okay, I need to get home and have a stiff drink or four before tomorrow. You two are more than welcome to come for a visit, like right now."

"Oh, no." Nick laughed. "Nothing but love for you, Mom, but you are on your own there."

"I'm going to pretend I don't hear this conversation about my parents," Nick's father said wryly.

As they were getting into their car, Beth saw Declan walking Ella toward her car. She urged Nick to leave quickly to give them some privacy. Maybe this would be the night that Ella's dreams came true as well. Of course, she also couldn't deny that the phrase *Be careful what you wish for* kept running through her mind as she worried about Ella's situation.

Chapter Twenty-two

Beth walked up to the receptionist's desk on Monday for her usual morning chat with Ella. The depressed expression on her friend's face told her all she needed to know. Smiling brightly, Beth said, "Hey, girl, how was your weekend?"

Ella gave her a wan smile in return. "It was all right. I really enjoyed the wedding. Do you know where Suzy and Gray went for their honeymoon yet?"

"Nick said they are in Bora Bora."

"Wow," Ella gasped, clearly impressed.

"Yep. As long as they have a beach, my sister will be in heaven. You would think she'd get tired of the ocean since she practically lives on top of it. So, how did things go with Declan Saturday night?"

Ella laid her head in her hands and sighed. "The dance was wonderful and we talked, but I felt like he wanted to walk away the whole time. I caught him looking at me funny a few times so I tried to ask if he had something on his mind. He said he was thinking about something at work. I just don't understand why he suddenly won't talk to me anymore. I have gone over and over it in my mind and I can't think of anything I said that would have offended him."

"Oh, Ella, I don't think you said or did anything. I saw him looking at you Saturday night and he clearly feels something toward you. What, I don't know, but there is something there."

"Well, what should I do?"

Giving her friend a hug, Beth said, "I know you don't want to hear this, but do nothing. Declan is nervous or scared of something. Give him some time and space. When he does come around, be friendly. See if you can get back to a comfortable relationship with him. Don't ask him for anything, most of all for a date. You need to see if he will let his guard down again."

"Geez, maybe life was easier when I was clueless about men. It's hard to play all these games. I have bought every book and every magazine and I still don't know what I should be doing," Ella admitted.

Beth hid a smile behind her hand. "I know it's hard, and I'm far from an expert. I don't have much more experience than you do. Nick is my longest relationship ever. Before I met him, I had never been involved with anyone more than a month. I wish I could tell you that it will get easier."

"It is easier for you now with Nick, right?"

Beth pondered Ella's question. "Hmmm, well I guess parts of it are. I'm comfortable with him and he's a straightforward guy. There are times he still puzzles me though, and I know I confuse the hell out of him."

"Oh, great. When do things get easier, then?"

Beth laughed. "If you're lucky . . . never!"

Beth worked her ass off for the two weeks that Suzy was on her honeymoon. She went into the office early and fell exhausted into bed every evening. The one positive was that she had replaced her morning sickness with sex. Since she barely saw Nick in the evening, she made sure she woke him in the morning.

Her hectic workload had also made it easier to manage her eating. Several days, she worked straight through lunch without eating. Her stomach continued to round slightly, but the scales remained stable.

Nick had caught her in a lie the previous evening. Since she was no longer eating in the evening, she hadn't bothered to check the usual staples in the refrigerator. Nick had come home earlier than usual and had asked if she wanted to go out to dinner. She told him that she had already eaten. When he asked what she'd eaten, she said a ham sandwich because she always kept that for a quick meal. She could still remember his next words, "Hmmm, really? We've been out of sandwich makings here for a week."

She had tried to play it off. "Oh, I know. I have been meaning to get by the store. I just picked a sandwich up on the way home since we didn't have anything here." She could tell by the look in his eyes that he didn't believe her. She had changed the subject, asking when Suzy and Gray were due back and he had let it go. She had noticed his eyes on her a few more times during the evening. She was ashamed to admit it, but that one night she had used sex to distract him.

Chapter Twenty-three

"Oh, God, can't I even be back at work for a day without being called to a covert meeting?" Suzy complained.

Nick hugged his new sister-in-law, not put off in the least by her abrupt manner. He knew that Suzy was a ton of bark and, luckily, only bit when she had to. "Oh, come on, you love it. It must have been rough being out of the loop for the last couple weeks." When an unusual blush colored Suzy's face, he rolled his eyes. "I know how much you like to share, but please spare me whatever you are thinking because the man is my brother."

"Tsk, tsk, jealousy is so last year, Nicky. Now that you dragged me out of my house early this morning, get to the point. I have a ton of crap lined up at work, so our tea party will have to be fast."

"It's Beth."

"Well, duh. I assumed it was since you didn't want to invite her and tell her that we were meeting. So, what gives? Did she throw you out? Just suck it up and say you're sorry."

"That's not it. She . . . I don't think she's eating, Suzy."

Giving him an impatient look she said, "Come again?"

"I think she's skipping meals and lying about it."

"Why would she do that and how do you know?"

Nick shifted in his seat, wondering where to begin. "I think it all started with the dinner with your parents a few weeks ago, when your mother and father were going on and on about her weight. She acted as if it didn't bother her, but I think it hit a panic button somewhere inside her. At first she told me she was eating earlier to avoid getting sick in the mornings, which sounded reasonable. Then I noticed that anytime we were together for a meal or snack, she would pick at it, but never really eat more than a few bites. I still just put that down to her not feeling well.

"Suzy, she just doesn't look healthy now. Last night she told me that she had a sandwich for dinner and then when I mentioned that we were out of sandwich makings, she looked really funny and said she had gotten the sandwich on her way home. When I was going to push it further, she ripped my clothes off to change the subject."

"Oh, shit, must you go there every time? Can't I be around you two without having to talk about your sex life?"

"Yeah, sorry about that. I was trying to make a point."

"Well, how about making it with less detail next

time? I have already been scarred for life by the crap I know about you and my sister." Suzy rubbed her temples as if a headache was brewing.

Nick hated to pounce on her on her first day back to work, but he needed backup. "Will you just talk to her today and see what you think? I hope I'm wrong, but I have a bad feeling about it."

"I'll see if I can feel her out without her knowing that you said anything to me. She might kick you out for real then, buddy. So, how are things between you since the whole baby-on-board thing?" she asked.

Nick smiled, completely at ease. "We are good. I'm happy about the babies, and I think Beth is starting to get excited, too. She actually bought a few baby books, so that's a start."

"Okay, good. We can stop right there before you move on to intimate details that will have my coffee screaming back up my throat." Then, squeezing his arm, she added, "Thanks, though, for telling me. I'm glad you're watching out for Beth. As you know, we only have each other, and with her being pregnant, I could use the help."

Nick drove off feeling guilty for talking to Suzy behind Beth's back, but he was also relieved. If Beth was in trouble, Suzy would sniff it out and take care of it. He was damned glad to have Gray and Suzy back.

"Holy scarecrow, when was the last time you ate?" Suzy demanded as soon as she saw her. *So much for subtle. Damn, I shouldn't have blurted that out like that, but look at her. I leave for two weeks and return to a sister who looks like a stick figure. I hate to admit it, but Nick is right. There is a problem here.*

Beth laughed as she settled into the seat in front of Suzy. "What are you talking about?"

Suzy rubbed her temple again, feeling the headache that had begun during her conversation with Nick pick up momentum and start to pound. It was like the end of vacation and the beginning of hell. "You look sick. Have you been to the doctor lately?"

"Nope. I have to go again next week. Why?"

"Are you still getting sick a lot? You look ill."

"Well, thanks. Do you have any more compliments for me?" Beth snapped.

Suzy took a deep breath and tried to be something she had little experience with: gentle.

"I'm just worried about you. You look like you've lost weight since I've been gone. Are you eating?" Suzy didn't miss the defensive look on her sister's face or the squaring of her shoulders.

"Of course I'm eating. What is it with you and Nick? Why does everyone assume I'm skipping meals? You know how often I have thrown up since I've been pregnant. If I'm thinner, it's for that reason and nothing more."

Yep, classic denial. Thank you so much, Mom and Dad, for causing this big old mess. Did you have to screw with your daughter's head? Hey, let's give you another award for parents of the year. "Beth, I know the parents said some crazy shit to you at my house and I hope that you didn't believe it."

Beth stood up and gave her a blank look. "I don't even remember, sis. Let's just forget about it. I need to make some calls and I know you have a ton of stuff to do so I'm going to let you get to it. We can catch up later. I'm glad to have you back."

When Beth pulled the door shut behind her, Suzy knew that her sister had never been less happy to see her. Despite all the work that littered her desk, Suzy swung her chair toward the window behind her and wondered how to help Beth when she so clearly didn't want it. She wanted to call their parents and tell them off, but what good would it do? They would never believe that they had done anything wrong. Facts and figures were their life and there wasn't room for anything outside that. If she told them that they had contributed to Beth's eating problem, they would roll out the statistics of women with eating and mental disorders. There was simply no room in their lives for emotion or guilt. Suzy was eternally grateful that they had chosen a work conference over attending her wedding. At least everyone was able to enjoy it without them ruining the day.

Tapping a pen on her desk, she tried to think of ways to help her sister. Beth had seriously pissed on the talking option, so what was next? An intervention? *Yeah, that will go well. Maybe we could all lecture her and stuff food in her mouth. Ah, hell. There were certain times in everyone's life when being an only child would rock, and this was one of those times.*

Beth leaned weakly against the door of the restroom stall. She felt dizzy and frail. She had rushed to the restroom thinking she was having a delayed bout of morning sickness, but so far, nothing had happened. She wobbled over to the sink and wet a paper towel to wipe her face. Her skin was clammy and she couldn't decide if she was hot or cold. The cell phone in her jacket pocket went off, sounding like a bomb exploding in the quiet restroom. She fumbled and finally pulled it out. Pressing the button to answer the call, she sighed in relief when she heard Nick's voice. "Hey, princess. How about lunch with a hot stud today?"

"Nick."

"Um, yeah. Who were you expecting? Is there another hot stud that you lunch with?"

"Nick, I . . . I'm sick."

Suddenly all the teasing left his voice, as he demanded, "Where are you?"

"Bathroom," she choked out.

"I'm coming, baby. Is anyone with you?"

"No. Hurry, Nick, I don't feel good."

"Hang on, I'm on the way. If you aren't sitting down, princess, then do it before you fall down. Shit, are you in the restroom on your floor?"

"Ye— Yes."

"I'm in the stairwell now. I won't take the elevator because we would lose our connection. Are you sitting down?"

"Mmm, hmmm."

The restroom door started opening and Beth vaguely recognized a woman from the advertising department as she started in. She looked surprised at Beth sitting on the floor. Suddenly, Nick flung the door open and ushered the woman back out. He ran over to Beth's side and squatted on the floor. "What's wrong, baby? Are you hurt?"

"Just sick, Nick."

"I'm going to take you to the hospital. Put your arms around my neck while I pick you up."

"No hospital. Please take me home. I'm just dizzy. It's morning sickness." Beth could see the uncertainty play across his handsome face. "Please, Nick, I'm okay. I just need to rest for a while."

He trailed a gentle finger down her pale cheek before gently lifting her into his arms. "All right, princess, but if you aren't feeling a lot better soon, we're going straight to the hospital. Understand?"

Beth laid her cheek against his hard chest, grateful to have him to lean on. When had she started depending on him to take care of her? She knew in her heart that Nick would protect her with everything that he had, just as he would their babies. Why was she resisting being a family with him? He might not love her, but he would love their children, of that she was certain. *You may never admit it to anyone else, but admit it to yourself. You love him. No, no, no! Oh, God, no!* There was nowhere left to hide. All of the denial in the world wouldn't change the fact that she had fallen in love with Nick Merimon, just as countless women before her had.

Now the dizziness that she felt had nothing to do with being sick. She risked a quick glance at his face, hoping he hadn't noticed the sudden tension in her body. He could never know how she felt about him or it would be over. Worse yet, he would stay because of the babies, but she would have to live with his pity. She couldn't be another woman who pinned all her hopes and dreams on landing him. She knew that he wanted her and they both genuinely enjoyed each other, but never once had there been any mention of feelings. *How could I have been so stupid? I let him in.*

They were attracting a lot of attention as Nick carried her from the building to his car. She knew that Suzy would know within minutes and would be frantic. As soon as she finished that thought, her cell phone trilled. Without looking at the caller ID, she handed the phone to Nick. She heard him assuring Suzy that he was taking care of her and not to rush after them. After a few more moments spent convincing her, Nick handed the phone back to Beth, and said, "Please don't do that to me again. Your sister just made some new and disturbing threats that involved certain body parts and sharp instruments."

Beth laughed weakly, still trying to shake off the

shock of the realization that she loved him. She felt like it was plastered on her face for the world to see. Luckily, he didn't seem to notice anything out of the ordinary. "Still okay, princess? We can go to the hospital now."

"No, please, let's just go home. I feel a little better."

Without further argument, Nick had the car in gear and was soon carrying her into the apartment. He settled her on the couch and grabbed a pillow and a blanket to wrap her in. "Have you eaten this morning?"

At that point, she was too tired to lie to him and too hungry to care if she gained a pound from a meal. "No, I was planning an early lunch." *So maybe that was technically a lie, but she would have had something to eat, right?*

He pursed his lips in disapproval and said, "I'm going to see what I can find. Call me if you need anything."

Beth closed her eyes and was soon drifting off. She startled awake when she felt a hand pushing her hair back from her eyes. Nick was perched on the coffee table in front of her with a tray containing some type of soup and crackers. "I'm sorry; this was all I could find. When you're settled and feeling a little better, I'll make a run to the supermarket and stock our shelves." Her stomach rumbled from the mouthwatering aroma of the soup. "It's just chicken noodle," Nick said, "but it was that or rice cakes so I took a chance."

"It smells amazing; thank you." She sat up against the cushions and Nick settled the tray on her lap. Any other time she would have been embarrassed at how fast she consumed the bowl of soup, but once she started, she couldn't seem to stop. It was the best meal she could remember having in ages and she ate until the tray was clear.

Nick gave her a smile of approval when he removed the empty tray. "Good girl." He took the tray to the kitchen and she was surprised when he came back to the couch and lifted her up so that he could slide in behind her. When he had her settled in his arms to his satisfaction, she snuggled into his warmth. His hands settled on her temples and she moaned in bliss as he rubbed them gently. The combination of the meal and the massage was more than her tired body could handle. Within moments, she felt herself slipping away. How could love be any better than what she felt right now in his arms? It was just the icing on the cake. She could live with this. It was enough, wasn't it?

Chapter Twenty-four

Beth lay in his arms sleeping peacefully, but sleep wouldn't come for Nick. So many thoughts swirled in his head. He had little doubt that her sickness earlier was brought on by not eating. She had devoured the soup as if she hadn't eaten in a week, and she probably hadn't. What was he going to do with her? He couldn't force-feed her, but his days of accepting her word that she had already eaten were over. It was time to make things more difficult for her to try to cover up skipping meals. He would stop going to the gym in the evening. Making sure she was okay was more important than working out. Come to think of it, he would start matching his office hours to hers as much as possible. He could work at home in the evening if he needed to. If they rode to and from work together, she couldn't say that she had picked up something on the way home.

He was worried about what she was doing to the babies, but he was more terrified of what she was doing to herself, mentally and physically. Not for the first time, he longed to strangle her uptight parents. What must they have put his beautiful girl through in her life to make her feel this way? His gut clenched as he imagined something happening to her. He couldn't comprehend a world without Beth in it. Somewhere along the way, she had become home to him. They laughed together, they played together, and she could drive him to the edge with just one look. There were moments he wanted to kiss her and moments he wanted to strangle her, but the one thing stayed constant: the want. They might not have the white-picket fence or traditional relationship like Claire and Jason, but they could come pretty damn close.

The only problem left was how to convince Beth of that. Was she truly ready to be a family—with him? He knew women wanted love, hearts, and roses, and he could give her two of those three things. Wasn't that enough? It was more than a lot of people started off with or ever had.

The ringing of Nick's cell phone made him cringe. He knew without looking who it was. Which body part would she threaten this time? He felt sorry for Gray, the poor bastard. He was likely to have his dick cut off sometime during his life unless he kept his wife happy. He had pissed off a few women in his lifetime, but none that made the colorful type of threats that his new sister-in-law made. Sadly, he knew she wasn't bluffing.

"Hey, sis, what's shaking?" *That's real wise, Merimon. Go ahead and piss her off. She will be over here with a knife and a pair of scissors before you can say "balls."*

"I'm not your sis, doofus. How is Beth? Oh, and thanks for calling me back."

"Save some of that charm for my brother. Your sister is asleep and seems fine now. I think she just went too long without eating."

"Shit! I tried to talk to her today, but she got pretty pissy with me. You're right though, there is something wrong with her."

"Excuse me," Nick taunted. "Could you repeat that part about me being right again?"

"Yeah, yeah, shut-to-the-up and let's figure out what we're going to do, pretty boy."

He really hated to admit it, but he was crazy about his new "sis." She was rude, crude, and irreverent, but funny as hell. Even with the constant threats of bodily harm, he could see why Gray fell so hard for her. "I'm going to make it hard for her to skip meals. I plan to change my schedule around so I can keep an eye on her more. I do have to go to Charleston tomorrow, but I'll come back instead of staying over. We have an appointment next week with her doctor, and I hope they give her hell if she has lost weight."

With a deep sigh, Suzy said, "Oh well, I guess it's a starting point. When you aren't around, I will force her to go to lunch with me so I can keep an eye on her. I can hit the Krispy Kreme every morning on my way in and buy a few dozen donuts to tempt her. Of course, I'll probably get attacked on the elevator before I even make it to the office with them."

Nick chuckled. "That sounds like a plan. Why don't you swing by here and pick her up on your way to the office tomorrow? I need to leave early and I don't want her driving until we know that she's okay."

"Yeah, no problem. Just let her know. Um . . . thanks, Nick, I really appreciate you looking after her."

"Oh, man, I bet that hurt. You don't need to thank me. Beth is, well, you know . . ."

Suzy laughed. "Yeah, I do know, Nick. The question is, do you know?"

With that parting shot, she was gone. What the hell was she talking about? Maybe she had taken to drinking at the office. That would explain a lot.

Beth could barely remember anything from the previous evening. She seemed to recall Nick coaxing her to eat more food before she stumbled into bed. Apparently, she had been more tired than she'd thought. He had woken her briefly before he left, saying he was going to Charleston for Mericom for the day and that Suzy was picking her up in a few hours. She had tried to argue, but he was adamant.

She expected the worst when she stepped on the scales after eating more than normal the previous day, but she was pleasantly surprised to see that she was down a pound. This day was already starting out better than yesterday. She pulled on her new standard pregnancy attire: a dress. She needed to go shopping for some slacks that she could wear. She was starting to dress like Ella before her makeover.

Suzy burst into the apartment without knocking and walked into the kitchen.

"I know I gave you that key, but could you please knock before barging in? You almost made me pee my pants."

"Ewww, must we go there this morning?" Suzy groaned. "You know, since you got knocked up, I'm hearing entirely too much about bathroom issues, horniness, and the whole 'I'm gonna cry any minute' thing."

Beth laughed at her sister's martyr expression. "I'm sure this is tough on you, but your understanding and your compassion mean so much to me."

Suzy made a face and flipped her off. "Are we ready here or what?"

"Yep, lead the way." Beth followed Suzy out and locked up. God, how did her sister wear her platform shoes as easily as someone wears a pair of running shoes? Beth liked her high heels, but she had to draw the line at anything that would land her on her ass. She climbed into her sister's SUV and strapped on her seat belt, and they were away like a shooting star. When they suddenly pulled into the parking lot of an IHOP, she looked at Suzy in surprise.

Shrugging her shoulders, Suzy said, "What? I missed breakfast this morning since I had to come pick you up and I'm starving. I love their Grand Slam Breakfast."

"Yeah, right. Denny's has the Grand Slam Breakfast, not IHOP."

Suzy grabbed her hand and pulled her toward the door. "I just call them all the same thing, eggs are eggs, right?"

Beth hid her grin as Suzy walked over to a booth and plopped down as if she were a regular. The table full of men beside them almost fell out of their seats. Suzy flashed them a big smile and went back to looking at her menu. When the waitress walked up to take their order, Suzy said, "We'll both have the Breakfast Sampler, coffee, and juice."

"Bu—but I was going to have fruit," Beth stammered.

Suzy raised an eyebrow at her and then turned back to the waitress. "We'll take some fruit with our breakfast."

"So, is this some Make-Beth-Eat thing?" she asked.

"I don't know what you mean. Can't a girl have some breakfast without the third degree?"

Beth had to give her sister props; when the mountain of food arrived, Suzy dug in as if it were the best meal ever. Much to the delight of the men at the next table, she even licked syrup from her finger. Suzy also watched like a hawk as Beth ate. "Is there something wrong with your food?"

"No, I'm just not used to eating such a heavy breakfast; it might make me sick."

Suzy took another big bite of her pancakes and said, "Well, I've got all day, so take your time."

Beth had a bad feeling that they weren't going anywhere until she put a dent in the huge mound of food in front of her. She started with the eggs, thinking they had the least number of calories. When Suzy still looked ready to camp out for the duration, Beth moved to the bacon and one of her pancakes. She wasn't lying when, a few minutes later, she pushed her plate back and said, "Please, Mom, I'm full. I can't eat another bite."

Suzy gave her a satisfied smile and pushed back her clean plate. "Now, that wasn't so bad, was it? That will tide us over until lunch. I'm thinking Mexican food or some nice buffet somewhere, what do you think?"

I think I'm in trouble.

Operation Feed Beth seemed to be well under way. How in the world was she going to keep from gaining ten pounds this week with her sister determined to eat like a lumberjack for the entire day or, hell, probably the entire week?

Nick smiled when he pulled in front of the house that he could find with his eyes closed. There wasn't one bad memory that he could associate with the place or the woman inside. She kept him grounded, and he loved her more than his own life. The smile on his face got wider as he rang the doorbell and waited for his first love to answer. When the door opened, he knew he was home.

"Hello, Nicky-boy. Fancy seeing you here."

Nick enveloped his mother in a bear hug, twirling

her lightly in the foyer. "Hey, Mom. I guess you've been expecting me, huh?"

She held up the spatula and motioned him in. "After you, baby boy."

Nick walked into the kitchen and smiled at the array of bowls sitting on the center island. Gray had a fondness for red velvet cake, but Nick was a chocolate man. He could make a mean chocolate pound cake and his mother knew it. He pulled an apron from the drawer in the island and grabbed butter, eggs, and milk from the refrigerator.

His mother sat quietly while he mixed his dry ingredients. Finally, he broke the silence saying, "So, I guess you were surprised to find out about Beth and the babies."

She laughed quietly and said, "Well, your father was shocked as hell, but me, not so much. I knew something was going on with you, Nicky. I always know when something is different with you or your brother."

Flashing a smile, he asked, "How do you do that? We never could get anything past you. I always thought you had about ten sets of eyes that were constantly swiveling."

"Oh, honey, a mother just knows. You and your brother are creatures of habit, and when that changes, it's a pretty big tip-off that something new is happening. With Gray, every time he went to Danvers in Myrtle Beach, he came home glowing. Within a few days, he was trying to find reasons to go back again. His moods were all over the place. I knew he was in love. I was just waiting to see who the woman was. As different as they are, Suzy is his true north.

"The first tip-off with you was the break in your dating pattern. You have always loved the ladies and they have always loved you," she said fondly. "Ever since the merger with Danvers, you continued to travel between Myrtle Beach and Charleston frequently because of the, um . . . connections that you have here. When you stopped coming home, I knew there was a woman involved. Of course, that sex dial confirmed it."

Surprised, Nick jerked his head.

"Oh, please, Nicky. I wasn't born yesterday. Pick some better excuse than butt dialing me while you were working out. If there was a gym around with moaning like I heard on that phone, I'd be a lifetime member!"

"Oh, God. Mom, please don't go there."

"What? I'd take your father too."

"If possible, that picture is even worse." Nick groaned.

"All right, As I was saying, I knew you were involved with a woman and I figured it must be different if you were staying in one place. She is different for you, isn't she?"

"Well, sure, Mom; she is going to be the mother of my children."

"That's not what I mean, Nicky, and you know it."

Suddenly defensive, he kept his head down as he

poured his cake batter into the pan. "It's not the same as my brother, so don't even go there. I care about Beth, but we aren't a great love story like Suzy and Gray."

"Ah, my sweet, dense boy. I see you are in the second stage of grief."

"What are you talking about?"

With a sympathetic smile, she said, "The three stages of grief are: shock, denial, and acceptance. You need to get past your denial stage and move on to acceptance."

"Mom, I have no idea what you're talking about. Do I need to check the dessert wine?"

"Nicky, you are grieving over your old life. It's a big change to go from being a confirmed bachelor to having babies. You have to be reeling from the shock."

The spoon in his hand clattered to the floor as, stunned, he looked at his usually rational mother. "I'm not in love with Beth and I'm not in some stage of grief. I fully accept our relationship and that we are going to be parents. I think I'm doing pretty well at accepting the change. Why would you think that I love her? You've barely even been around us together. I don't 'do' love—you know that. I don't love her, I don't!"

His mother continued to sit there, giving him a pitying expression. *Why was everyone so sure that he felt something that he didn't? I guess if you get a girl pregnant, everyone wants to believe that you fall instantly in love and together you ride off into the sunset. Hell, now his own mom was on the deluded train as well.*

"I'm not going to push you, Nicky, but I know I'm

right. The next time you're with Beth, just think about how you would feel if she moved on with her life—without you."

"I don't think that's likely to happen, Mom—we are having a family together."

"No, Nick. She's having your children. That doesn't automatically make you a family. Beth could move on, marry someone else, and you could become a weekend father. How would you feel about another man raising your children full-time while you took a part-time role?"

For the first time in his adult life, Nick yelled at his mother. "No one is taking my family!"

"You really mean that no one is taking Beth from you, don't you? Honey, I don't want to upset you, but I do want you to realize, before it's too late, that you aren't guaranteed a life with Beth unless you're ready to give her everything she needs and deserves. You deserve it, too. Just don't close your mind to the future. If you can't imagine Beth not being in your life every day, then you need to make sure that you give her a reason to stay—before it's too late."

Nick dropped his head to the counter, while his mom ruffled his hair as she had when he was a boy. "Stop sulking and get the cake out of the oven; I think we both need some chocolate."

Chapter Twenty-five

"Please don't make me go to IHOP again tomorrow morning," Beth begged. Suzy had insisted on having their morning meeting over breakfast for the entire week. If she never saw another piece of bacon, it would be too soon.

"What? I think it's been good to shake things up a little bit. Besides, Bonnie enjoys seeing us every day," Suzy said, referring to their regular IHOP server.

"I'm not stupid." Beth huffed. "I know what you're doing. Suddenly you're making time for breakfast and lunch every day and a snack, and Nick hasn't missed dinner since he got back from Charleston. You've got Operation Feed Beth in full swing."

"Full of yourself much?" Suzy laughed. "If you must know, I'm working off a lot of calories every night being a newlywed and all so I have to put some of them back on during the day. Marathon sex really takes it out of a girl."

Despite herself, Beth couldn't contain the giggle that slipped out. "You're full of it, but I'm gonna stop there before you insist on telling me any graphic details about your nights. I need to be able to look Gray in the eyes without further intimate knowledge of him."

"Ah, suit yourself. Intimate knowledge of Gray is the best kind. That man has so many talents."

"Why, sis, that sounded almost dreamy."

"Oh, bite me," Suzy snapped.

"Wow. I knew you would come begging, but I never thought it would be in front of your sister."

Beth whirled in her chair to see Nick leaning against the doorway with his usual sexy grin. *Is it wrong that I want to jump on him, roll him down the hallway, and rip his zipper open with my teeth?* She only half listened as he continued to trade barbs with Suzy. When Beth's gaze finally locked with his, she could tell that he knew exactly what she was thinking. Shifting uncomfortably in her seat, she tried to look away before Suzy noticed the heat between them.

Nick cleared his throat and asked, "Are you ready to go, princess?"

"Um . . . I just need to finish up a few things with Suzy."

Waving her hand toward the door, Suzy said, "Uh, please, just go. I can't get anything done while you make puppy-dog eyes at each other. Just don't make out in the damn elevator, please. I have to ride in that thing."

When Nick smirked and opened his mouth, she held her hand up to stop him. "Forget I said the word *ride*."

With a satisfied grin, Nick shut his mouth and followed Beth out the door.

"So, where to for dinner, princess? How about Italian?"

Did these people ever miss a meal anymore? She felt like she spent her entire day, every day, planning her next meal. She had given up getting away with not eating breakfast and lunch. Suzy watched her like a hawk, so there was no hiding anything. Nick, however, was a different story. As long as they ate at home, she could get away with eating very little. She distracted him using a usual male weakness: ESPN. She insisted on eating in front of the television, saying it was more relaxing and, being a guy, he couldn't turn it down.

She was ashamed to admit that she had resorted to hiding food in the couch cushions and going back later to throw it away. Within a few minutes of settling in front of *Sports Center*, Nick was totally oblivious to everything around him. She could pop out a boob and he wouldn't notice. As long as she stuck with food such as sandwiches, which were easily slipped under a cushion, he was none the wiser. He didn't say anything, but she knew he was happy when he looked at her empty plate.

Part of her knew that it was wrong, but what could she do? She was eating more than she had been, so couldn't everyone just be happy about that? The scales showed that her deception was working. Despite the meals during the day, she was still maintaining her weight. Instead of being filled with dread, she was actually looking forward to tomorrow's doctor's appointment. The number on the scales would be something to be proud of for once.

"Hellooo? Italian?" Nick asked again.

Oh, crap. How am I going to get around that? Even if we get takeout, it's going to get messy hiding spaghetti or pizza in the couch. Think fast . . .

"Hey, what about the place down the street, Manzoli's? I don't want pasta, but they have great subs. We could get it to go. Wasn't there a game on that you wanted to watch tonight?"

Nick beamed his approval at her. "Good idea, babe."

I'm a rotten person. The man is looking at me like I'm a rock star while I plot to buy a sub that will fit under the cushions without causing too much mess. The acting award for the most convincing liar goes to Beth Denton!

Beth woke to a hand gently rubbing her stomach. At first, she thought that Nick was trying to wake her up in the way that they both enjoyed. She wasn't sure why she didn't move to let him know that she was awake, maybe curiosity. When his hand didn't move past her stomach, she was intrigued. He caressed the slight swell of her belly softly, almost reverently. His fingertips explored every inch, as if memorizing her new shape.

Normally, this type of scrutiny would have made her uncomfortable, but something was different in his touch. There was nothing sexual, nor did she feel like he was having any negative thoughts about her changing body. The opposite seemed to be true. She lay there while he explored her for what seemed like hours, but was probably only minutes. Just when she was planning to move, signaling that she was awake, he leaned over her and softly kissed her stomach. She held her breath and tried to will away the tears that were gathering in her eyes. She was thankful when he slid out of the bed and walked to the bathroom, shutting the door behind him.

What had just happened was so out of character for the Nick that she knew. His actions made it appear that he was happy about her pregnancy. But he never really mentioned it other than asking her how she was feeling, so she assumed that he was in denial. Now she had to wonder if Nick was handling her pregnancy better than she was. Did he think he would freak her out if he talked about the babies or showed excitement? Was she depriving him of her pregnancy by trying to protect him? Maybe it was time to stop acting as if it wasn't happening and see where Nick stood.

Pregnancy was supposed to be one of the most exciting times in a couple's life. Just because Beth and Nick weren't married didn't mean it couldn't be that way for them as well. After her doctor's appointment, she would drag him into Babies "R" Us and see how he took it. She had to smile at the image of a ladies' man like Nick in a baby store, where he would either sink or swim.

Chapter Twenty-six

When they were settled into the waiting room at the ob-gyn's office, Nick looked around and whispered, "These women here hate men."

"What are you talking about?" she whispered back.

"Just look around. Most of them are giving me evil looks. Is this like when you have a baby and you start screaming obscenities at the father because you're in pain?"

Trying to hide her smile, she said, "Yeah, maybe." She didn't bother to add to his inflated ego by telling him that most of the women were looking at him as if he were the last piece of cheesecake on a buffet. Let him continue to think they were staring for a different reason. He would probably send one of them into labor if he turned his sexy grin on them.

"So, how about breakfast after this? We left home before we had a chance to eat."

Beth couldn't contain her groan. "Could we at least get through an hour without someone mentioning food?"

Nick gave her an innocent smile that didn't fool her for a minute.

"Beth Denton."

They both stood as the nurse called her name. As if trained, Nick walked past the scales and to the end of the room. She almost called him back since she was pleased with what she knew the number would be, but thought better of it. If she had lost any weight, he wouldn't be happy about it and would redouble his efforts to feed her.

The nurse frowned as she recorded the number. "You are two pounds lighter than your last appointment. Have you been experiencing morning sickness?"

With a rueful smile, Beth said, "Yes, I have."

"Well, make sure you replenish your fluids, dear. You can talk to the doctor about taking something to lessen it."

Beth gave Nick a bright smile as the nurse led them into a room and helped her up onto an examination table. He gave her a puzzled look, clearly expecting the same response she'd had at her last weighing in public. When the doctor came in a few moments later, she asked about her morning sickness and Nick mentioned her dizzy spell from last week.

"That can happen in pregnancy if you don't have regular meals and snacks. You have to remember that your body is processing food faster and it's easier to have dips in insulin levels." Nick shot her a smug grin as she promised the doctor to eat small meals throughout the day. "Now, if you would lie back, we will listen to the babies' heartbeats. The Doppler should pick them up now."

Nick stepped closer as if fascinated. "You can actually hear the heartbeats through that?"

The doctor smiled, charmed as everyone seemed to be with Nick. "We sure can." Then the doctor put the small probe against Beth's stomach. Soon, a loud, galloping sound filled the room. The doctor smiled as Nick jerked in excitement. Beth found herself lost in the moment as well, moved to tears at the evidence of the lives she carried. The doctor frowned and continued to move the probe as if searching for something. "I can only detect one of the heartbeats, which happens. Sometimes it can be hard to get in the right position to hear them both. Just as a precaution, I'm going to send you for an ultrasound."

Both she and Nick turned to the doctor in alarm. "Is . . . Is something wrong with the babies?" Beth asked.

"It's just routine, Miss Denton. When you're pregnant with twins, you're followed more closely, plus I'm sure you would enjoy seeing your babies again."

Nick gave her hand a reassuring squeeze as he helped her up from the table. She could feel her body trembling as she walked down the hall to the ultrasound room. Despite the doctor's reassurance, she was terrified, and she could tell that Nick was as well, despite how much he tried to hide it from her. She hadn't realized how much she wanted these babies until she was faced with the thought of losing them. *Oh, God, please let them be okay. Please God, please.*

The ultrasound technician was overly cheerful, as if trying to set their minds at ease. Nothing would do that though until she saw that both babies were fine. When the black-and-white screen came to life and the technician started looking at different angles, Beth held her breath. Nick gripped her hand tightly, as if he were on the verge of a nervous breakdown. When the technician removed the probe and stood, Beth knew something was wrong. "I'm going to get the doctor to check this, if you will excuse me for a moment."

Beth turned to look at Nick. "Something's wrong, isn't it?" She could see the effort it took for him to smile as if he wasn't worried.

"I'm sure it's nothing, princess. Just harder to see two babies than only one. Please relax. I will have you at a breakfast buffet before you know it."

The doctor came in alone and took the seat that the technician had vacated. Beth asked her the question she had asked Nick. "Is something wrong?"

The doctor didn't answer right away. Instead, she continued to look at the monitor as if searching for something. Finally, when Beth was certain she wasn't going to answer, she removed the probe, but left the lights dimmed. "Miss Denton, the ultrasound shows only one fetus."

"So why did you think I was carrying twins?"

"Miss Denton, you were carrying twins. I'm afraid you have experienced what we call vanishing twin syndrome."

Nick stood up, still holding Beth's hand. "What exactly is that?" he demanded.

"It's when two heartbeats and fetuses are detected on your first ultrasound, indicating twins, and on your next ultrasound visit, one no longer exists. Due to doctors requesting ultrasounds earlier in pregnancies, this is detected much more than it used to be."

Beth sat forward and, in a panic, grabbed her stomach. "But where is my baby? How could it just not be there? It's only been a month since my last appointment."

The doctor laid a hand on her arm, trying to calm her down. "Miss Denton—Beth —since it was so early in your pregnancy, one twin was just reabsorbed by the other one. There is little evidence when this happens that the other twin ever existed, other than the first ultrasound."

Choking back tears she asked, "Did I do something that caused this to happen?"

The doctor looked at her in sympathy and patted her hand again. "No, Beth, there is nothing you did that caused this to happen. The usual cause is a chromosomal defect. It's nature's rather harsh way of handling a pregnancy that isn't viable."

Seeing Beth's agitation, Nick sat back down beside her and gripped her hand. "What about the remaining baby?" he asked. "Will Beth have problems with the pregnancy?"

"Everything looks perfectly normal with the baby you are carrying. Since the loss of the twin happened in your first trimester and you had no bleeding or cramping, there is no reason to believe that your pregnancy won't continue on normally." The doctor rose to her feet and said quietly, "I'm going to give you some privacy. When you're ready, the nurse will bring you to my office and I can answer any other questions you might have. Please take all the time you need."

When the door shut behind her, Nick helped Beth off the table and pulled her into his arms. She stood stiffly, unable to feel anything other than the darkness that was descending on her. Sensing her detachment, he pulled back to study her face. "Honey, it's going to be all right. Let's get through this and then we'll go home."

Beth turned vacant eyes on him and said, "I caused this. I've hid, lied, and avoided eating, and I starved one of my babies to death to keep from proving my parents right. I killed our baby, Nick. What kind of person does that? I was supposed to take care of them, but all I could think about was myself. What kind of mother does that? You should hate me; I hate myself."

She saw Nick's face pale as he started shaking his head in denial. "Stop it. You didn't do this. You heard what the doctor said—this happens so much it has a name. Don't do this to yourself. Let's go talk to the doctor and she can tell you that you didn't cause this."

Beth pulled her arm out of his grip and walked to the door. "I'm not going to talk to the doctor; I'm going to the car. You can go if you want to. Hurry, though. We need to eat on the way home. I'm not going to starve my last baby, like I did my other one."

"Beth . . . princess." Seeing that there was nothing he could say at this point that would get through to her, Nick handed her his car keys and told her he would be out after he talked with the doctor. As she walked out the door, he slumped back into the seat.

Nick dropped his head as tension raced through his body. "Fuck!" What in the hell had just happened? He had barely recovered from the shock of finding out they were no longer having twins when Beth threw him for an even bigger loop. The blank look on her face threw him more than the doctor's words had. She truly believed that she had killed one of their babies. The look on her face went beyond grief. It was the look of someone who had become their own judge, jury, and executioner. She had found herself guilty of something so heinous that she couldn't deal with it without shutting down.

He knew in that moment that pushing her to voice her fears to the doctor was hopeless. At this point, she wouldn't believe a word that anyone said. He should probably be grateful that she mentioned breakfast, but somehow that only made things more eerie. Someone in a normal frame of mind would be too upset to think of food. For Beth to want to eat now, after what had just happened, gave credence to her belief that she had starved her baby to death.

Getting to his feet, he opened the door and followed the nurse to the doctor's office. She probably assumed that Beth would be coming back to accompany him, but he didn't see the need to explain it to her. He would tell the doctor about Beth's eating problems and, hopefully, get some reassurances from her that it had not affected the babies. At this point, he would never admit anything otherwise to Beth. Whether the doctor knew it or not, Beth was so fragile that one more blow might break her, and that was something that he could never allow to happen, even if he had to save her from herself.

When he left the doctor's office and settled in the car beside a still-quiet Beth, he, at least, had answers that he could share with her when she was ready to listen to them. He would give her a few days to deal with her grief. They both needed that. He was more upset than he could have imagined. Somewhere along the way, he had gotten very possessive of Beth and the babies and it was a huge blow to realize that there were no longer two babies. Yeah, he could give her a few days, but after that, she was going to listen to him. After they had a meal that he no longer had any desire for and after Beth was settled, he would call Suzy to get her support, too.

Beth would probably want to take a few days off.

Everything was going to be fine. *Really? Then why don't you believe it?* He only had to look at the stiff profile of the woman sitting next to him to know that, despite his pep talk to himself, it wasn't going to be a simple matter to bring her back to herself again.

Chapter Twenty-seven

"It's been a week, Nick. What is going on over there?" Suzy demanded.

Nick ran a hand over the back of his neck, trying to ease some of the tension gathering there. "Nothing has changed, Suzy. She eats, she drinks, she walks around the block, and then she goes back to bed. She takes care of every basic need that the pregnancy book tells her to and then she blanks out until the next meal."

"Have you tried talking to her again?"

Releasing a pent-up breath, Nick snapped back, "Of course! I talk to her constantly. She either gives me a one-word answer or ignores me. I fix her meals, fix her snacks, trail her on her walks . . . and I might as well be invisible. If I mention anything about the doctor's appointment and it not being her fault, she walks off. I thought she was grieving, but she never cries or shows any emotion. It's pretty damn scary."

"Screw this; I'm coming over. You need help."

"No, Suzy, please don't. The last time you were here, she locked her door for the rest of the evening, which drove me up the wall. We just need to give her some more space. She's eating and taking care of herself so we can't risk upsetting her right now."

"Shit, yeah, okay. I'll give you a few more days, but this can't go on forever. I'm worried about her."

"I know you are. So am I. I'm just trying to keep her calm. It hasn't been that long since we found out, so she just needs more time."

Beth ate on autopilot. She didn't taste food anymore; she didn't care what it was. The only thing that mattered was saving the baby that she still carried in her womb. If not for that, she felt sure she would curl into a ball and never come out again. The only emotion she felt was anger at herself. The sorrow had dimmed as the blame intensified. Had it been a boy or girl, before she ended its life?

The one thing she could remember about the doctor's appointment now was how proud she had been of losing weight. All those weeks of denying herself had seemed worth it as the number on the scale flashed. How far would she have gone if her appointment had been a few more weeks away? Would she have starved both babies in her paranoia of gaining weight?

Nick tried to tell her that it wasn't her fault, but surely he must blame her. He had to be lying to reassure her. A part of her knew that she was being unfair, but that fairness no longer seemed important to her. Her life now revolved solely around taking care of this pregnancy. She didn't want to return to work, she didn't want to talk to friends or family, and she only tolerated Nick because he took care of the things that she wasn't willing to, like grocery shopping and anything that would require her to rejoin the outside world.

She vaguely remembered Suzy coming by. Just as Nick had, she'd tried to reassure her that she wasn't to blame for the loss of the baby. Beth had tolerated her until her sister had finally given up and gone away. After that, Beth had locked the door, afraid of who would be visiting next. She didn't want pity, sympathy, or understanding. No one understood what she was going through or where her head was, and it pissed her off when they acted as if they did.

When the baby was born, she would leave Myrtle Beach and relocate somewhere away from all the prying eyes. Nick could go back to his old life and she would raise the baby on her own. Who would really miss her? Suzy had her life with Gray now, and her parents certainly wouldn't shed a tear. Just thinking about them made her body burn with rage.

If there was anyone other than herself that she blamed, it was them. They had set the wheels in motion and she, unfortunately, had followed right along behind them. She was finished with trying to win their approval. She fully planned to never see them again, and knowing their level of parental involvement, it wouldn't be a hard plan to carry out.

She loved her sister, but Nick would be the hardest one to walk away from. In those moments when her resolve wavered, she missed being in his arms. After the first few nights, he had given up sleeping with her and had taken spare blankets from the closet and slept on the couch. She expected him to pack his bags any day . . . and leave. Their whole relationship was based on sex, so why was he still here? Maybe some misplaced sense of guilt.

The days had long since started to blur together and she no longer knew how long she had been away from work and her regular life. Her focus was on the baby she carried. She laid a palm against the noticeable swell of her stomach. No longer was she concerned about the number on the scale. If she was never as thin as she was before her pregnancy, it didn't matter. She ate regular meals and made sure that she nourished the life within her.

Beth walked to the bathroom and looked at the reflection in the mirror. She barely recognized the woman looking back at her. Her face was pale and devoid of makeup. The long tank top she was wearing hugged her stomach and left little doubt that she was pregnant. Her yoga pants were the only thing she could still wear besides her dresses and tops. None of her slacks would button any longer, and she didn't care.

When the bedroom door slammed behind her, she squared her shoulders and hardened her heart. No matter how much she missed him, she couldn't let Nick see her weakness toward him. It was better for them to both make the break and move on.

"Is this a private pity party or can anyone join?" Beth spun around to see Suzy with her hands on her hips, standing in the doorway. "I'm really surprised you haven't put up some black curtains or started burning incense."

"What . . . How . . . did you get in?"

"Well, your guard has also lost his mind, so I snuck in while he was gone. He's probably getting himself chewed up and spit out."

Wary now, Beth asked, "What're you talking about? He went to the store."

Shaking her head, Suzy said, "Oh, no, he's not. He is gone to protect his princess from the root of all evil: our parents."

Beth walked back into the bedroom and fell heavily onto the bed. "Why would he go see them?"

Rolling her eyes, Suzy said, "Gee, I don't know. Perhaps because they pushed the woman that he loves off the deep end, and he blames them for everything."

"He blames them?"

Suzy flopped on the bed and asked, "Out of that whole sentence, you only picked up on the blame thing?"

"I heard the rest, but Nick doesn't love me," she said dismissively.

"Oh, God, was I as stubborn as you are? The man wouldn't have done half the crazy shit he's done if he wasn't in love with you. Wake up!"

"Suzy, I really don't feel like arguing over this. All he has done is fix some meals and walk with me. How does that spell love? I could probably pay the guy from Domino's to do the same thing."

"Beth! The man hasn't been to work in weeks. He shops for you in the middle of the night after you go to sleep so you won't need anything while he's gone. He has refused to travel so Declan is doing most of it. He sold his Audi and got an SUV with a car seat. He bought a damn baby monitor and hid it in your bedroom so he would hear you if you need him. He has parenting books stacked to the ceiling in the living room and he hasn't shaved in weeks. The entire family divides their time between worrying about him and worrying about you."

"I . . . I can't believe that," Beth whispered.

"Well, you better believe it. You need to get out of whatever funk you're in and help the poor guy. He's grieving, too, and you are shutting him out. He needs you, sis. You know men are horrible at this crap."

"He has really gone to see Mom and Dad?"

Suzy fell backward on the bed in defeat. "Boy, you are fixated on that part, aren't you? Yes, I think he's there right now. He called Gray this morning, seriously pissed off. He has been stewing on the things they said to you. He said they needed to know what had happened and that if they didn't clean up their acts, they wouldn't be a part of the baby's life."

"I can't believe he's doing that."

"No kidding. The man means well, but they are

probably chewing him up and spitting him out right now." Suzy pulled Beth down beside her, hugging her tight. "I'm so sorry, sis. This whole thing just sucks."

Beth allowed Suzy to pull her close. It felt so good to be with her sister again. They lay there in comfortable silence for what seemed like hours until Nick's voice startled them both.

"Any other time, this moment would have been a dream come true," Nick said, as he motioned to them in the bed with their arms around each other. "Now that you're married to my brother and are like an annoying sister, this just seems wrong."

With a sniff, Suzy sat up and said, "In your dreams, Nicky. So you survived a parental visit without any visible wounds. I'm impressed."

Nick's eyes were locked on Beth as he answered Suzy. "Yeah, I think we reached an understanding."

Suzy looked at Nick and her sister, and hopped off the bed. "So, I think I'm going to head out. Gray will be wondering if I'm working a street corner again." When neither Beth nor Nick showed any surprise over her last sentence, she smiled. "No, please stop begging me to stay. I told you, I have things to do." When she still got no reaction, she walked toward the bedroom door. "Call me when you two come up for air." With another smirk, she was gone.

Nick couldn't take his eyes off the woman in front of him. She was now standing before him, looking like

Beth again. Her eyes were no longer empty. Instead, an emotion that he hoped was love shone from them. She looked young, fragile, and beautiful. The deep breath he took stuck in his throat when he saw her hands resting against the curve of her stomach. She usually wore a jacket when they walked so he hadn't noticed the evidence of her advancing pregnancy. He felt his legs go weak at the miracle growing inside her. Dropping to his knees, he placed his hands over hers and tears blurred his vision. Lowering his head, he laid a tender kiss on her stomach.

"Ah, princess. Please tell me you're back, because I can't stand to lose you again."

Beth dug a hand in his hair, rubbing his head soothingly. "I'm here, Nick. I . . . I just need you to hold me for a while."

Nick gathered her in his arms and settled them on the bed. She spooned against his front while his arms came around her, linking gently over her stomach. His lips trailed down her neck as he breathed in her familiar scent. How he had missed having her in his arms. He never wanted to go to sleep or wake up again without her lying beside him.

He took a deep breath and hoped he didn't scare her away. "So I know Suzy told you I went to see your parents today." He felt her nodding against him and he continued. "I talked to your mom and dad for quite a while. I told them how damaging their comments on your weight have been to you. I also told them about our loss and, you may find this hard to believe, princess, but they were devastated."

Beth jerked around to look at him. "No way. That's not possible, Nick."

"Honey, it is. It seems that my words to them that night at Suzy's had gotten them thinking. I'm not saying that they have suddenly became Ward and June Cleaver, but they want to do better. I don't think they really know how to be typical parents, so it may be a long road."

"I don't want to see them!" Beth said fiercely.

"I know, princess, and they aren't going to push you. Let's just file it away for another day, okay?"

He felt Beth relax against him. "They still insisted on calling me Nicholas or young man, though. Well, except for when I was leaving."

Beth started giggling. "They were so glad to get rid of you that they slipped and said, 'Good-bye, Nick'?"

Smiling, Nick said, "Nope. When I told them how much I loved their daughter, your father said, 'Take care of my girl, son.'"

The room was deathly quiet and Beth had gone stiff in his arms. Maybe he should have tried a more romantic declaration of love. "He called you *son*?"

Nick pulled her around to face him. "You did catch the other part, right?"

Beth gave him an innocent smile, saying, "I don't believe I did. Could you repeat it?"

He smiled at her indulgently as he said, "I love you,

Beth Denton. Please be the woman by my side, the mother of my children, and the siren that I adore for the rest of our lives."

Next, Nick pulled Beth on top of him and asked, "So, do you have anything to tell me, princess?"

Beth looked down at him just as her stomach growled. "I'm hungry?"

Nick dropped his arms in defeat. "Oh, God, I give up."

Laughing, Beth lowered her lips to his and teased her tongue along his mouth's seam. Just as his lips parted, she pulled back and said, "I love you, too, Nick. I was afraid I would never be able to admit that to you, or even to myself. But I do love you, so much. There is no one else on this earth that I would rather have as the father of my baby than you."

Nick reached up and cradled her head with his hands to finish the kiss that she had started. Food was soon forgotten as they made up for the weeks they had been off course. Nick tried to take it slow but Beth urged him deep inside her as she wrapped her legs tightly around his hips. He was powerless to deny her anything and soon his hips were pumping in a hard rhythm. His heart melted as she told him several more times how much she loved him. Would he ever get tired of saying it or hearing it?

He now knew he had spent his whole life going from woman to woman never involving his heart because it was already taken. He was born to love this woman in his arms and to be the father of the child she carried . . . and all of the other children they would have. No matter where they were, she would always be home to him.

Beth snuggled against Nick as they ate a late dinner on the couch. She even turned on ESPN so he could watch football while they ate. She admitted that she had been hiding food in the couch. Nick paused with his slice of pizza hovering near his mouth. He dropped the pizza back to his plate and turned off the television. Pulling her onto his lap, he rested his forehead against hers. "Ah, baby, I had no idea. I wish you could have talked to me about what was going on in your head."

A tear rolled down her cheek at the emotion in his voice. "Me too, but I couldn't. It's still hard. I . . . I have a problem, Nick. I would like to think that the trauma of what happened has cured me, but I can't be sure. The fear has always been there just below the surface since I lost the weight. I could blame it on my parents, and they do deserve some of the blame, but not all of it."

"Talk to me then, princess. Tell me why you feel the way you do because I see nothing but beauty regardless of what size you are."

With a sniffle, Beth took a deep breath and admitted, "I've never liked myself. For a big part of my life, I was overweight and disgusted by the reflection in the mirror. I became so obsessed at avoiding mirrors that I only kept a small one to apply makeup. I avoided seeing my full body; it was too horrible. Finally, several years ago, I went to the mall to buy a dress for a friend's wedding. The dressing room was made of floor-to-ceiling mirrors. Suddenly, I could no longer escape the person looking back at me. I begged out of my friend's wedding and, from that moment on, I only ate enough to get by. There was nothing healthy about the diet I put myself on, but it worked. I lost the weight and I lost it fast. If I thought my parents were critical before, it got even worse. They badgered me about regaining weight. I completely stopped eating in front of them. I moved out of their house and got my own place just to escape their scrutiny."

Nick rubbed her back and waited quietly for her to continue.

"I finally found a happy balance with food. I found if I exercised every day, I didn't have to exist on just the bare minimum. No matter what number the scales showed though, I still cringed every time I stood in front of a mirror. I wore small clothing sizes, but I still felt like one meal could change that immediately. I have lived in terror of gaining back the weight—as my parents predicted—and of never regaining control."

"The pregnancy pushed you to the brink, didn't it?" Nick asked quietly.

"Yeah, it did. When I found out, that is all I could think about: that I would gain weight and destroy everything I had worked for. I was still doing okay though, until that dinner with my parents. That pushed me right off the deep end. Having them voice all my fears, and pound away at my hard-won confidence snapped something inside me. From that moment on, my entire focus was avoiding food. I lied, I hid it, I did everything short of gagging myself, and I'm not sure how far away that was. I'm scared to know what the breaking point would have been for me, Nick."

"Beth, you didn't cause what happened. I told the doctor everything and she assured me that, although it could have caused you problems eventually, your diet had nothing to do with vanishing twin syndrome."

"I know, but in the back of my mind I will always wonder, and there is no way to change that. It was a wake-up call that I never wanted to happen."

"I hope this doesn't make you mad, but I have been doing some research and there are some great groups in the area for people with eating disorders." When Beth opened her mouth, Nick held his hand up and continued. "I would go with you, princess. You don't have to decide right away, but I want to help you."

Seeing Nick visibly braced for her answer made her heart melt. "Thanks, baby. I think that's a good idea. I do have a problem and I can't continue to believe that I can handle it on my own. I don't want to pass on this type of body-image problem to our children. I need to learn to like myself."

"Princess, you need to learn to love yourself, just as I love you. I love you for you. Whatever size you feel comfortable with is for you to determine. I never want you to think you have to resort to starving yourself for me. You are Beth to me, not a number on the scales."

Beth wrapped her arms around Nick and wondered how it was that every painful moment in her life had brought her to this point. She might have a long road ahead of her, but with Nick by her side, the only thing that was important was the ride.

Chapter Twenty-eight

Beth climbed in Nick's new SUV and buckled her seat belt. They usually rode to work together a few days a week when they had the same schedule. Tonight they were going to dinner before heading home. When Nick turned away from the city, Beth looked around curiously. "Where are we going?"

"I have to run by Gray's. I still have his garage door opener and he's raising hell about it."

"Why didn't you just give it to him or Suzy at the office today?"

"Oh, I just forgot. So we'll drop it off and then go to dinner."

Even for Nick, that was a strange explanation, but Beth had learned long ago to just go with it. Suzy probably sent him a nasty text message and threatened some other body part if he didn't return it immediately. When they pulled in a few minutes later, she stayed in the car, thinking Nick would just run it in and they would be on their way. When he opened the door for her, she looked up in surprise. "I can just wait here."

"No, come on in for a few minutes. I . . . I need to go to the bathroom."

Oh geez, have we reached the point in our relationship where we talk about our bathroom habits? "Well, okay. I guess I can wait inside." Nick took her hand and pulled her into the kitchen. When he turned around and swung her up in his arms, she thought he had lost his mind. "Nick, what are you doing?"

He sat her on the counter and stepped back. Was it her imagination or did he look nervous? "Princess, you know I love you."

My God, is he going to break up with me in my sister's house? "Yeah, I know, and I love you, too."

"Good, good," he said, fidgeting. "So most people spend anniversaries where they had their first date. They, um, also do other things where they had their first date."

"Okay, sure." *Why does he look so terrified?* When he suddenly dropped to one knee, the breath left her body. *Oh my God!*

"Beth, I'm worried that we didn't have our first date in a more romantic location, but since this is where it all started, then it had to be the start of the rest of our lives together. I love you more than I ever thought it was possible to love someone. My life was empty until you stormed into it. Please do me the honor of being my wife and the mother of my children. Also, please protect me from your sister's threats for the rest of our lives."

Nick pulled a ring box from his pocket. He opened

FALL FOR ME   271

the box, revealing a large princess-cut diamond ring sparkling against black velvet. He was looking at Beth as if his life depended on her answer.

Beth was crying, but she managed to nod her head, and then yelled, "Yes!" Nick slid the ring onto her finger and pulled her from the counter and into her arms. "I love you, Nick." Beth sobbed as he twirled her in his arms.

When he placed her back on her feet, she pulled back and asked, "How in the world did you get Gray to give you his kitchen again?"

Nick laughed. "It wasn't easy and I had to promise not to compromise the counters again. He said Suzy was going to the gym after work so she wouldn't find out until it was too late. Apparently, she hasn't forgiven us for our first 'date' in her kitchen."

"Yeah, I still regret telling her that. She sure does hold a grudge." Then, placing her arms around his neck, she said, "Of course, if that should happen again, I would never make the mistake of telling her."

"Princess, I don't think that's a good idea . . ."

Beth pushed her body closer to his, running her hand down lightly and grazing his growing erection. "I don't know what you're talking about."

"Ahhh, baby, don't look at me like that. You know I have no control where you are concerned. We need to get out of here."

"If Suzy is going to the gym, she'll be a while. Where is Gray?"

Nick was having a hard time forming words with her hand stroking him through his slacks. "Ugh, drinks . . . client."

"Perfect," she purred.

"Ah, hell," Nick moaned as he lifted her back to the counter. "If your sister ever finds out about this, I'm blaming it all on you."

Beth choked on a laugh as Nick lifted her shirt and started to suck on a nipple through the thin fabric of her bra. All thoughts left her mind as they re-created their first coupling on her sister's granite counter. It was hot and furious. The possibility of getting caught made the thrill even greater. When it was over, Nick collapsed against her while Beth leaned against the cabinets and panted.

"That was freaking amazing," Nick wheezed.

Beth stroked her fingers through his thick hair, nodding her agreement. Who would have thought that what began in this kitchen would eventually bring them full circle here? When she had given in to her desire for Nick Merimon in this very spot, she never imagined that she would be the woman to tame the playboy. She had no doubt in her heart that he was completely hers, body and soul. What she ever did to deserve him, she didn't know, but she liked to believe that one of the stars she had wished upon so long ago had finally heard her plea.

Nick shifted off her and helped her off the counter. "We'd better get it together and get out of here." He pulled up his slacks and zipped them, leaving his dress shirt hanging out. He pulled Beth's shirt down and helped her button her new maternity slacks. Beth knew that eating in a restaurant was no longer an option. It was going to be takeout. They both looked like they had just made out in the backseat of a car.

Giggling like teenagers, they walked out the kitchen door and ground to a stop as Suzy stood in front of them with her hands on her hips. Beth heard Nick groan as she gave her sister a sheepish grin. "I know you two horny goats didn't just deface my kitchen yet again!"

"Well . . . we were just leaving your garage door opener," Nick offered.

"Really? So you broke in and had sex in my kitchen so you could return it?"

"Not exactly. Gray knew we were coming so we didn't break in," he defended.

Beth winced, as Suzy's voice got higher. "Gray said you could have sex in our kitchen?"

Nick looked at her and stepped back. "I'm sorry, princess, but I told you that this one was on you if we got caught, so good luck."

Beth rolled her eyes as he stepped behind her. "Coward." As Suzy glared daggers at them, the door slammed and Gray walked in. He appeared to assess the situation in one glance and gave a wry grin.

Suzy turned toward him with an innocent, sweet expression. "Baby?"

"Yes, dear?" Gray answered.

"Did you tell your brother that he could make out in our kitchen again?"

"Um . . . not exactly."

Beth stepped forward and shoved her ring finger in her sister's face. Since both men seemed to be terrified of her, she thought it was time for a distraction. Suzy's mouth curved into a smile as she looked at the engagement ring.

"Well, I'll be damned. I have no idea why you needed to return to the scene of the crime for this, but congratulations! Nicky, couldn't you have at least taken my sister to a nice restaurant to propose?"

Nick looked at Suzy sheepishly and said, "This was our first . . . date, so it had to be here. I was planning to take her somewhere nice afterward."

Suzy and Gray hugged them both. With a dramatic shudder, Suzy said, "If you will give me a minute to get my rubber gloves and Clorox out, I'll grab us a drink from the kitchen to celebrate." Suzy walked gingerly to the kitchen wrinkling her nose in distaste.

Gray clapped his brother on the shoulder and said, "You do realize when you two are on your honeymoon, Suzy and I are going to christen every surface in your apartment."

Beth could feel her face turning red as Nick snickered. "Sorry, Gray," Beth mumbled.

Gray laughed softly, "No worries, Beth. Welcome to the family. I'm happy for you guys and so is Suzy. She just needs to recover from the shock of another kitchen violation."

Suzy returned from the kitchen with a tray of drinks. Beth drank her glass of apple juice as everyone else sipped a glass of wine.

Suzy cleared her throat and raised her glass. "Congratulations, baby sister. Nicky is a handful, but I know you can manage him. May you have everything you have always wished for. Gray and I are here for you and, with the exception of babysitting, we will help with anything that you need. Our home, with the exception of the kitchen, is always open to you."

Beth smiled as she looked at her sister leaning with such contentment against Gray. Nick stood beside her with his arm curved around her waist and his hand resting against the swell of their child inside her. It hit her in that moment that this was it. This was what she and Suzy had searched for their whole lives: a family. Despite being told repeatedly that they didn't exist, they had found their Prince Charmings. From this moment on, it was no longer Suzy and Beth against the world. They were part of the Merimon family where dreams were encouraged and anything was possible.

I have no idea what I've done in my life to deserve the love of the man beside me or the support of the family surrounding me, but I have it. I feel it. I'm completely in love with everyone in this room and for the first time in my life, I'm falling in love with me as well.

Epilogue

"Princess, it's going to be fine. This is our second ultra-sound since . . . The last one was fine and we've felt the baby kicking."

Beth wrapped her arms around Nick's waist, allowing him to pull her into an embrace. "I know, but I don't think I'll ever not be nervous." Their follow-up ultrasound last month had been normal and the baby was right on schedule. They hadn't been able to see the sex of the baby since he or she had stubbornly kept his or her legs closed. They were having a 3-D ultrasound this morning, and she was both excited and terrified to see the baby.

Nick had been wonderful and, outside of pushing her to get married, he had been more than she could have ever hoped. He was fully involved with every area of her pregnancy. He pampered her, he worried about her, and he treated her exactly like the nickname he used for her: princess. He was ready to get married as soon as possible, but she wanted to enjoy being engaged and to plan the girly wedding of her dreams.

They had also attended two meetings at Eating Disorders Anonymous. Nick had been incredibly supportive and he knew that each day was a struggle to accept the number on the scales. It would be a lifelong process, but she was happy with the progress that she had made.

Nick brushed a kiss on her forehead and led her out of the apartment and to the car. Another thing that Nick had been pushing for was buying a house. He was scared that she would fall on the stairs, and she had to admit that they were getting taxing. She promised him that they would start looking soon. He wanted a house on the beach and, although she loved the ocean, she still enjoyed living in the city and having everything nearby.

She felt the familiar tightness in her chest as they walked into the doctor's office. She signed her name and took the seat beside Nick. He wrapped his hand around hers and whispered, "These women in here still hate me."

Beth smiled because she knew that, as usual, they were checking out her man and ogling him like a piece of candy. When her name was called, Nick squeezed her hand reassuringly and followed her to the ultrasound room. He helped her onto the table and whispered in her ear, "I love you, princess," before sitting down. No matter how calm he tried to act, she knew he was nervous, too.

She was vaguely aware of the bubbly technician

chatting, but her eyes were glued to the monitor, waiting to see signs of life from the blurry image. When she saw the image of their obviously active baby, Beth let out a breath that she didn't know she had been holding. Nick pressed his lips against her temple as they both gazed in wonder at the beautiful 3-D image.

"Ohhh," said the technician.

They both jerked their eyes to her, alarm evident on their faces.

"Do Mom and Dad want to know the sex of the baby because it's quite obvious," the technician teased.

Unable to speak, they nodded their heads in agreement. "Congratulations, it's a boy!" The technician pointed to what looked like an extra arm and Nick started chuckling.

By now, Beth's silent tears had become more of a loud sobbing. Nick handed her some tissues, but couldn't tear his eyes from the picture of his son, who appeared to be attempting some in-utero acrobatics. The technician handed them pictures and a DVD to keep, then left them alone in the room. She probably thought they needed to get control before they saw the doctor.

Nick helped her from the table and pulled her down into his lap. "Thank you, princess."

Surprised, she asked, "For what, honey?"

"For giving me this moment, for loving me, and for carrying our baby. I can't think of another time in my life when I have been this happy or this content."

Beth stroked her hand down the face of the man she loved and said, "It's my pleasure, Mr. Merimon. Heavy emphasis on the pleasure part."

Beth dropped her fork on her plate with a contented sigh. Nick had insisted on breakfast after their doctor's appointment and she was more than happy to join him. The doctor had been pleased with the ultrasound, and the baby continued to measure on target. Nick paid their bill and took her hand as they crossed the parking lot.

"You know, princess, since we're having a boy, I would like to name him after my grandfather, my mother's father. I was crazy about him. He died when I was ten. I know he would love for my son to carry his name."

"I think that's a great idea. I know it would mean a lot to your mom. So, what was his name?"

Nick kicked the ground with his shoes, refusing to make eye contract.

"Honey, what was his name?"

"Herman."

"Um, what?" Beth asked, thinking she had heard him wrong.

"Herman."

She closed her eyes and shook her head. "Honey, I love you, but I'm not naming our child Herman. Didn't he have a middle name?"

Nick continued to look down and finally muttered, "Winston."

Beth jerked around in surprise. "Your grandfather's name was Herman Winston?"

"Yeah. We can call him Hermie, for short."

Beth looked at him incredulously. "You think that sounds better than Herman?"

"It's fine, princess. It's just a name; what's the big deal?"

"It is a big deal. I'm not having our son beaten up in school all the time for having the name Herman Winston. Did his parents not like him?"

Nick put his hands on his hips and glared at her. "Princess, this is half my son and I'm naming my half Herman. You can name your half whatever you want to."

Beth crossed her arms and glared right back at him. "Oh, really? Well, I think your half is already getting named Merimon so that leaves the other names to me."

He opened her car door and motioned her in. When they got in he said, "Buckle up, we're going to settle this the Merimon family way."

She looked at him in confusion, but buckled her seat belt, curious to see what he was talking about. *The Merimon way had better be pretty damn good if he thinks he's going to convince me to name our son Herman.*

Nick's mother looked surprised when she opened the door. "Well, hello, you two." Then worry played across her face as she studied their expressions. "You had your doctor's appointment today—was everything okay?"

Nick stepped forward to give her a kiss on the cheek as he ushered Beth into the foyer. "It was good, Mom. We found out we're having a boy."

His mother squealed and folded them both in a hug. "I'm thrilled, but you could have called me. You didn't have to drive all this way."

"We didn't drive here to tell you, we are here for your kitchen. Break out the cookware, Beth and I need to make a decision."

"Um . . . ok. Is there anything I can help you with?" his mother offered.

Nick sensed the perfect ally in his mother. She would surely back him on naming their son after her father. Maybe he could end this argument right here without ever entering the kitchen. "I want to name the baby after Grandpa Norton, but Beth doesn't."

Nick's mother gave her son a proud smile and then looked at Beth with a questioning look.

Beth squirmed as she tried to justify her decision. "Vicky, I think it's a wonderful idea, but I just think it would make it hard on the baby when he's older to be named Herman Winston."

Beth heard a chuckle as Nick's father joined the group. He hugged and congratulated them both. She was relieved when Nick's mother gave her a bright smile of encouragement before turning back to her son. "Nicky, I think you two need to bake this out. Go in the kitchen and suit up. You know that's where we solve our problems and make our decisions." Then, smothering a laugh behind her hand, she said, "Your dad and I will be there in a minute."

Beth let Nick pull her through the foyer, toward the kitchen. She couldn't understand why Nick's mother and father seemed so amused by their argument over the name. She was relieved though that Nick's mother no longer seemed offended by her desire not to name the baby Herman. She let Nick tie an apron on her and smiled when he also put one on himself. The man could even make baking look sexy. *Down, girl. You are already banned from your sister's countertops; don't repeat that mistake with your future in-laws.* Beth smiled and vowed to control herself, but she stood firm on two things: she was not naming their baby Herman and she was going to attack Nick Merimon as soon as they got home.

John Merimon looked at his wife as she dissolved in a fit of laughter. "Why does Beth think that Nick wants to name their baby Herman?"

"Oh, honey," Vicky said, laughing, "you missed the best part. Nicky wants to name the baby after my father, Herman Winston."

John looked even more confused as he said, "But your father's name was Henry, not Herman."

"I know, I know," she gasped. "Remember how Dad was always picking on the kids and calling himself different names and saying he was from different places? Well, apparently our son bought in to it. He thinks

Dad's name was Herman and he's determined to convince Beth to name their son after him."

John started laughing too after finally getting the joke. "He was pretty young when your dad died so I guess it never came up after that." Pulling his wife into his arms, he whispered in her ear, "So are you planning to tell them what your dad's name really was?"

Vicky leaned back in her husband's arms, with her eyes dancing in mischief. "Well, of course. Just as soon as they have those cakes finished. I'm a little hungry, how about you?"

John laughed as he squeezed her tight. "What difference will an hour make? I hope one of them is making lemon pound cake."

Author's Note

Thank you for purchasing *Fall for Me*. I hope you enjoyed reading it as much as I enjoyed writing it. I'd love to hear your comments. Please feel free to e-mail me at Sydney@sydneylandon.com or visit me at www.sydneylandon.com for updates on upcoming books. There are now six books tentatively planned for the Danvers series.

CONNECT ONLINE

www.sydneylandon.com
facebook.com/sydney.landonauthor
twitter.com/#!/sydneylandon1

Acknowledgments

Thanks to Jennifer at Hot Damn Designs for my cover art.

To Elizabeth Humphrey for editing. It's always a pleasure working with you.

A special thanks to all of my wonderful friends on Facebook, Twitter, Goodreads and Pinterest. It has been so wonderful getting to know you.

If you loved *Fall for Me*, don't miss
Weekends Required,
where it all began with Claire and
Jason's romance!
Read on for a preview of *Weekends Required*.
Available now wherever books are sold.

"Holy smoking buns, a butt like his should be illegal."
Claire looked up in time to see the object of her co-worker and best friend's admiration walk past their table in the cafeteria. Jason Danvers truly did have a butt to admire. At well over six feet tall with dark brown hair that tended to curl up at the ends, compelling ice blue eyes that looked right through you, and a rugged and tanned, athletic build, Jason Danvers was very hard to ignore. His presence always seemed to dominate a room. His every movement impatient, Jason never seemed to relax. Every lady in the cafeteria was craning her neck to get a better look.

"Suzy, keep it down before Mr. Smoking Buns hears you."

"Oh, puleeze. Don't tell me the drool isn't pooling in your mouth as we speak."

"Suz, you're too much— What's Jeff going to do with you?"

"Well, I don't know what Jeff has in mind, but I've

got thoughts of handcuffs and whipped cream, myself."

Claire had met Suzy on her first day at Danvers International, and it hadn't taken long to form a bond
with the outspoken, flashy, and hopelessly sex-obsessed
wisecracker. Suzy was what every little girl wanted to
grow up to be: gorgeous and confident. With long dark
red hair, a tall, slim build with curves in all the right
places, Suzy loved pushing the fashion envelope at the
office. She handled special events for Danvers International and, as she often told anyone who would listen,
she was damn good at her job.

Her boss had long ago given up trying to stress the
importance of the professional dress code to her and
now suffered in silence when Suzy showed up for work
in various forms of leather and lace or neon-colored
T-shirts with catchy slogans. Claire suspected that Suzy
was so beautiful that no one actually cared what she
wore, as long as they could admire her every day.

Claire considered today to be a subdued day for
Suzy, who was wearing only a blue-jean miniskirt and
a rainbow-colored shirt with a peace sign on it. She
often wondered how they'd bonded so quickly. Suzy
had a colorful and sexy fashion style, to say the least,
while Claire preferred a more tailored look. Classic
slacks and tops or pencil skirts in neutral tones were
her usual work attire. Whereas Suzy favored I've-just-
had-hot-sex hair, Claire's tresses were long, auburn,
and tended to curl when loose, so for the most part she

kept her hair pulled back from her face in a discreet ponytail.

Suzy also loved the tanning salons, even though Claire often lectured her on the dangers of that particular pastime. Wherever they went, men stopped to stare at Suzy, and Claire might as well be a picture on the wall or a potted plant for all the attention they paid to her. Suzy always begged Claire to let her do a make-over. Claire shuddered at the thought.

"I don't know how you work so closely with him without attacking him."

"I value my job, and I just don't think of him in that way—or any man for that matter right now."

"You're way too uptight. Live a little, Claire. You might actually enjoy it."

Thankfully, Suzy seemed to run out of steam in a relatively short time with her "live a little" pep talk, and packed up her tray. "Want to catch a movie later or check out the new bar on the corner?" Suzy asked.

"I've got to run over to Mom's to pay her bills for the month."

"One day you're going to have a wild moment, and I hope I'm still young enough to appreciate it," Suzy said with a dramatic sigh. "Okay, catch ya later—and don't do anything I wouldn't do with Hot Buns."

No matter what the differences between them, Suzy was a breath of fresh air in Claire's otherwise dull daytime routine. She laughed under her breath and thought to herself, *If Suzy had any idea what I was doing last night she would probably die of a heart attack on the spot.* She hoped that would be over before anyone ever knew the lengths she was forced to go to pay her mother's medical bills. She gathered up her own tray and headed to the front to drop it off.

"How're you doing today, my love?" George asked. George ran the cafeteria and had been with Danvers for thirty years, hired back in the day Marshall Danvers, Jason's father, started the company. George always had a smile for everyone and, in truth, a soft spot for Claire.

"I'm good, George. Thanks for asking."

"When are you going to let me take you away from all this?"

"Now, what in the world would Sara say, George?" Sara was George's lady friend, as he called her, and the two were just a perfect match.

"Sara would understand if I had to trade up. We got an understanding."

"George, you wouldn't even know how to get up in the morning without Sara. You better hold on to her with both hands. She's a keeper."

"That's true, but a guy can dream, right?"

"You're hopeless, George. You have a good day."

"You too, love. See you tomorrow."

Claire walked down the hall to the elevator bank. No corners were cut with the decor of Danvers International. Everything here was gleaming: white marble floors, soft off-white walls, and stainless steel elevators with mahogany walls inside. As she stepped into the elevator she once again forced herself to remain calm. Confronting her fear of enclosed spaces was what forced her to take the elevator every day instead of the stairs. While the stairs might be better for her physically, conquering her claustrophobia was far more important.

Danvers International was a huge glass-and-steel building with twenty-five floors. Jason Danvers's office was on the twenty-third floor, and his personal space was on the twenty-fourth and twenty-fifth floors. The door to Jason's large office was closed, as usual. Putting away her purse in the bottom drawer of her desk, she settled into her chair in the reception area.

Jason liked the office to be very impersonal and she was always careful to have no personal items on her desk. His one concession to some type of informality was to address her by her first name, and he liked to be addressed by his as well.

She had been working as Jason's assistant for three years. Her job generally required her to handle all the liaising with clients, suppliers, and other staff. She was Jason's right hand and ensured that all appointments, meetings, and projects were scheduled and staffed as needed. Her office life was never slow or boring. He was a fair boss and always treated her well. In the time they had worked together they had managed to create a comfortable relationship. It wasn't exactly a friendship, because they didn't have personal conversations. It was more of a mutual respect for each other's abilities.

She was checking her e-mail when the office door opened and he strolled out. His normally wavy brown hair was rumpled as if he had been running his hands through it, and his mouth was pulled in a tight line.

"Claire, could I have a word with you in my office?"

Normally he just relied on the telephone to give orders, so it was somewhat of a surprise to be summoned personally. He waited for her to step out from behind her desk and precede him into his office. Claire was initially surprised at how at odds Jason's office seemed to be with his personality. Jason was very direct and a person of few words. His clothing favored darker colors with his style usually expensive and conservative. At thirty-five years old, he could easily pass for someone in his twenties. His office, however, had a nautical motif. Jason had several beautiful colorful pictures of the ocean and various beach scenes, and the room was reminiscent of an expensive seaside hotel.

She had been shocked the first time she'd entered his office at how comfortable and soothing it was compared to the rest of Danvers International. She'd heard from various employees that Jason loved the sea, which was a major reason Danvers International headquarters remained in Myrtle Beach, South Carolina, rather than moving to a bigger city that would offer more benefits to a company of its size.

She'd spent a lot of time in this office imagining rolling around on the floor buck naked with her boss—carpet burns be damned! Just because Suzy was her best friend didn't mean she had to tell her that her fantasies of Jason were probably better than anything Suzy had dared to imagine. Carefully schooling her face into a neutral expression, she looked at Jason with what she hoped would pass for professionalism and not "do me" desperation.

"Claire, I need you to work this weekend. I know I usually don't impose a weekend work schedule; however, the contracts for Mericom are supposed to be finished on Saturday, and I'll need you to be on hand to handle any last-minute changes that may take place."

"That's not a problem. What time should I be in the office on Saturday?"

"That's the problem. Unfortunately I'll be going out of town this evening to Columbia, and I'll need you to travel with me. My friend Harold is getting married on Sunday, and I'm expected at his home for the weekend since I'm in the wedding party."

Oh, great. I've not worked weekends for over a year and rarely travel on business and now I'm being asked to do both!

"Jason, I have a previous family engagement for the weekend, but I'll be glad to be in the office during the day on both Saturday and Sunday."

"I'm afraid that isn't going to work. I don't need to remind you how big this deal with Mericom is to Danvers, do I?"

He had been working for close to a year on the acquisition of Mericom. Danvers International was the second biggest communications company in the United

States, and with the addition of Mericom, Danvers would move firmly into first place.

"No, that's fine. Would it be a problem if you gave me directions so that I could meet you tomorrow morning?"

"I guess that's okay. I'll e-mail the information to you shortly."

When Jason's cell phone rang, she took the opportunity to excuse herself from his office. *Crap, crap, crap. What am I going to do about this weekend?!*